"Tell me what you [...] moving to her other breast, taking it in his mouth and biting lightly

"Ohhh. My…" Charlene couldn't even finish the thought, let alone do what he'd asked of her.

"Do you want me to take your clothes off?" he asked, flattening his body against hers the best he could considering she was sitting in a recliner.

His broad chest brought a new sensation of heat against her midsection. His strength pressing into her thighs ignited the fire already brewing between her legs and she felt herself pressing into him desperately.

"Do you want to be naked?" His voice was more urgent now, strained with what she could only assume was desire. "You naked? Me naked? Me touching you, tasting you? Tell me, Charlene. What do you want?"

"Yes," she almost screamed, but it came out sounding more like a desperate whimper.

Books by A.C. Arthur

Kimani Romance

Love Me Like No Other
A Cinderella Affair
Guarding His Body
Second Chance, Baby
Defying Desire
Full House Seduction
Summer Heat
Sing Your Pleasure

ARTIST C. ARTHUR

was born and raised in Baltimore, Maryland, where she currently resides with her husband and three children. An active imagination and a love for reading encouraged her to begin writing in high school and she hasn't stopped since.

Determined to bring a new edge to romance, she continues to develop intriguing plots, racy characters and fresh dialogue—thus keeping readers on their toes! Visit her Web site at www.acarthur.net.

A.C. ARTHUR

Sing Your Pleasure

KIMANI
ROMANCE

To Julian Hawkins—
for having the strength to just be you.

 KIMANI PRESS™

Recycling programs
for this product may
not exist in your area.

ISBN-13: 978-0-373-86177-4

SING YOUR PLEASURE

www.kimanipress.com

Printed in U.S.A.

Dear Reader,

I fell in love with the title of this book from the very start. So in writing this story I knew that Charlene and Akil's love for music would set the stage for the love that would ultimately save them both. I listened to so many CDs while writing this: Trey Songz's *Ready* and Alicia Keys' *The Element of Freedom* were both at the top of the list. I think I wore out both CDs, lol.

But each disc seemed to capture the exact mood for this story—from Akil's volatile sexuality to Charlene's endurance and positivity. These were two people who really belonged together, whether or not they knew it or wanted to accept it. I am so glad I had the opportunity to share this story with you and hope you fall in love with Akil and Charlene, and, of course, the music.

Happy reading,

ac

Chapter 1

Moving from her closet to the bed where her suitcase was opened wide, Charlene Quinn sang the lyrics to "Finally" while folding and carefully packing clothes for her trip to Miami. The song was an oldie but goodie in her mind. The classic single by CeCe Peniston, released in 1991, hitting the number-one spot on music's *Billboard* charts, was a great dance tune that didn't quite give CeCe the credit her vocal abilities deserved.

Charlene couldn't stop playing the song. She had been since receiving the phone call two days ago from her agent, Sofia Wellesley of Limelight Entertainment. And while CeCe was actually singing about finally finding Mr. Right and falling in love, Charlene's rendition of the lyrics was something else entirely.

She definitely wasn't looking for love. Granted, she wasn't running from it either, like some people she knew, but it wasn't high up on her list of priorities. For Charlene, working as a vocal coach at the local community college was both challenging and rewarding because everybody who thought they could sing couldn't.

Her parents hadn't seemed thrilled with her career choice. They wanted her to be more like her older sister. Candis Quinn's illustrious career began with her debut as a Dainty Diaper Baby at the tender age of one. From that moment on, Candis had been in front of a camera, gracing the pages of magazines and then finally graduating to commercials in her high school years. Candis was three years Charlene's senior, and it was expected that Charlene would follow in Candis's footsteps.

It was usually around age three to four that most babies dropped the baby fat due to their increased mobility. Charlene's stuck like old gum to a shoe sole. While there were some ads that especially requested plump child models, the ones that wanted the cute, perfect look clearly outnumbered them. So Candis was the child star of the family.

Her father, Randall Quinn, had been the executive producer of over twenty hit sitcoms in the last thirty years. That made him the adult star of the family. Her mother, Marjorie, was the perfect wife, mother and overall female in Charlene's life. She supported her husband, went to all the photo shoots and commercial callbacks with Candis and tried her damnedest to make Charlene into something she just couldn't possibly be.

Marjorie had finally had enough of Charlene's diet failures when she turned sixteen. She took her daughter to a doctor, who quickly diagnosed Charlene with hypothyroidism, a condition described as a lack of functioning thyroid tissue and thyroid hormone. Early symptoms of this condition included fatigue, weight gain and water retention, all things that had plagued Charlene since she was a little girl. The strange thing was that this condition usually hit women during the first year after they'd given birth. Charlene's was a unique case, the doctor had said.

His diagnosis hadn't changed the stigma of growing up in Beverly Hills among models and actresses and a sister who was a goddess at five feet nine inches, boasting a teeny-tiny waist and sizable breasts. Even now, holding her own bit of height at five feet five and a half inches with a buttery complexion and slightly slanted brown eyes, Charlene felt a little uneasy about her looks. She was better than she had been but still the memory of being constantly ridiculed in school stuck with her. That's where her best friend Rachel had entered the picture.

Only three weeks ago Rachel Wellesley, the younger sister of Charlene's agent, Sofia, had been dealt a heavy blow. One of the things both she and Charlene feared had happened—Rachel had found herself in the limelight of the tabloids. Charlene met Rachel when they were both in the third grade attending the Beverly Vista School. It was there in the cafeteria, over a carton of warm chocolate milk and sticky, tasteless mac 'n' cheese, that a true friendship had been forged.

Like Charlene, Rachel came from a famous family— the Wellesleys, known for their budding new agency Limelight Entertainment. That, coupled with living in Beverly Hills, California, put the two girls in a position they dreaded. Paparazzi and reporters were always abuzz either around their homes or the school yard. Everybody wanted a glance into their personal lives, or at the time, the personal lives of their famous families. It was sickening and both girls swore they'd keep a low profile in their adult lives, which for Charlene wasn't going to be a problem since she didn't fit the profile of your average Beverly Hills female.

But the night she'd dragged Rachel to the karaoke bar in an effort to cheer her best friend up, Charlene's plans had changed.

"Why don't you sing something?" Rachel had said after the man with the beer belly and nappy-looking beard had shuffled off the stage. He'd attempted to sing "Flying Without Wings" by Ruben Studdard, but his rendition had been more than bad. Horrendous probably said it best.

"Oh, no," Charlene had answered quickly, taking a sip of her water with lemon slices. "You're the one on hiatus, you get up there. It'll do you good to get the whole situation with Ethan and the show off your mind."

Rachel was already shaking her head. "Now you know I can't hold a tune any better than I can hold hot coals in my hand. And the last thing I want to do is give the press any more ammunition against me."

Feeling the wave of sadness emanating from her friend made Charlene frown. She hated seeing the normally vibrant and cheerful Rachel this way. Reaching a hand across the table, she covered Rachel's. "It'll die down. You know those vultures find new targets every fifteen minutes. Besides, Ethan's love life is really old news."

Shrugging, Rachel tried for a smile. Unfortunately, the act was dismal and the smile never reached her eyes. "C'mon, Rach, I'm trying to cheer you up here. If you keep looking like that I'm going to get a complex. Being stuck with me can't really be that bad."

"You know what would really cheer me up?"

Rachel asked, this time her smile seeming a bit more enthusiastic.

Feeling the twinges of dread, Charlene responded, "What?"

"If you'd get up there and sing."

Her lips had been about to form the answer "no." Of all people in the world, Rachel knew how much Charlene loved to sing. She also knew all the insecurities Charlene kept from everybody else.

It was no secret that Charlene's passion was singing. She'd been singing any and every song she heard since she was four years old. It had been the only thing she was good at that Candis couldn't do. The best part about it was that Charlene could really sing. But once she had graduated from high school and went on to study music at The Herb Alpert School of Music at CalArts, furthering her musical knowledge, Charlene's focus had turned to training other people with musical talent.

But tonight wasn't about her, it was about the friend who'd been there for her through all her trials and tribulations. After all, that's what friends were for.

"If I do this, you'd better smile for the rest of the night. No more sulking, no more regretting, nothing. Deal?"

Rachel, knowing she'd won this not-so-small battle, smiled happily, turning her hand over to grip Charlene's. "I promise. C'mon, let's look through the catalog to see what songs they have."

Before Charlene could say another word, they were facing the computerized jukebox, pressing buttons that allowed the display of songs to change quickly. After about four screen changes, Rachel pointed to a song and proclaimed, "That one."

Reading the selection, Charlene couldn't help but

smile. It had been one of her favorite songs in high school.

So without further hesitation she'd selected the song and headed up to the stage while Rachel hurried back to her seat. It was Friday night, a little after ten, and the bar was just starting to pick up more customers. Karaoke night was huge here and the hot wings and beer weren't bad either. So as she adjusted the microphone to fit her height—the man with the huge belly had been taller by a few inches—she experienced a slight case of the butterflies after noticing the amount of people sitting at tables waiting for her performance.

Crowds bothered Charlene only to the extent that she didn't like people staring at her. As for performing, once she began singing she was often so lost in the music and the lyrics that all else ceased to exist. So her fingers trembled slightly when she lifted her enclosed fist to cover her mouth, clearing her throat.

Applause had already begun from a few of the customers sitting right up front.

"Sing, baby! Sing!" A partially inebriated man with a cigarette stuck to his lower lip yelled. How did he keep that thing on his lip? she wondered absently. Then she nodded to the older lady operating the karaoke machine.

She didn't need the words that appeared on the prompter, she knew the song by heart. The already dim room grew just a tad darker until there was only a spotlight on her. She couldn't see the faces of the people in the audience but could make out the outline of their heads. The first chords of music started and she felt that familiar stirring inside.

It began in the pit of her stomach, swirling around

until warmth filled her entire body. That's what happened when she sang, her entire soul was filled.

Then right on cue, with her eyes staring out into the darkness, she began to sing the lyrics to Mariah Carey's "Hero."

"There's a hero, if you look inside your heart. You don't have to be afraid of what you are." This had been her theme song all throughout high school. Of course it had been out for a while by that time, but it didn't matter. She loved the lyrics, loved what they meant and how empowered they made her feel.

Loved them so much that they were all she could focus on while singing and she didn't see the tall, slender man watching her from a table in the far corner of the room.

Ten minutes and a roomful of applause later, Charlene had stepped down from the stage, only to be stopped just as she approached the table where Rachel was still clapping gleefully.

"Jason Burton from Playascape Records. And you are?"

For a second she'd only stared at him, not even acknowledging the business card he held out to her with one hand or his charming smile. Had he said he was from a record company?

Then Rachel was by her side. "She's Charlene Quinn and I'm Rachel Wellesley from Limelight Entertainment Agency. How can we help you, Mr. Burton?"

The conversation had gone on from that moment but Charlene was so flabbergasted at the actual thought of this man thinking she'd sounded good enough to record that she barely remembered it all.

The next day Charlene and Sofia were in downtown Los Angeles riding the elevator to the executive offices of Sahari Davenport, CEO of Empire Music, the music conglomerate that distributed Playascape Records. Charlene had officially been signed as a Limelight client and with Sofia's smooth expertise had left that office two hours later with her first record deal.

And now, as if she hadn't been on a fast enough roller coaster of emotions, she was heading out to Miami to work with superproducer Akil Hutton, the man who was going to make all her secret dreams come true.

Something was wrong.

It just couldn't be, Akil Hutton thought for the millionth time since he'd received the package from Jason early yesterday morning.

"She's gonna be the next Whitney Houston, Ace. I'm tellin' you, wait till you meet her."

Jason had called him Ace since their early days interning at Empire. Over the last ten years he and Jason had worked their butts off to build this company into the hip-hop and R&B powerhouse it was today. They'd both started out as interns for Empire Music, knowing that one day they wanted a piece of that pie for themselves. Since Jason was a people person with a distinct ear for what was hot and what was not, he'd been a shoo-in for the A&R spot, "Artists and Repertoire" was like his middle name.

And since Akil had been more of a beats-and-lyrics man himself, he'd taken his seat in the studio, working alongside the engineers and the artists to get the perfect sound for each recording.

Nineteen number-one hits, seven platinum CDs, three gold, five Grammy Awards ranging from R&B Single to Producer of the Year and millions of dollars later, Akil and Jason were still hanging tight. Akil could say that Jason was the closest thing to a friend he had in this world.

And that was a sorry shame.

But back to this latest dilemma.

In one hand Akil held a picture, an eight-and-a-half-by-eleven glossy print of a pretty woman, with butter-toned skin and root-beer brown eyes. Her smile was fun, touching the soft dimples in each cheek and the edges of her eyes. Her dark hair was pulled away from her face in some sort of updo that didn't really flatter her other features. But that was the least of his worries.

Although her face had captured him, sent a little tinge to his chest, the rest of her made him pause. She wasn't a rail-thin woman—after being in the business for years he knew this was the look, slim and trim, almost emaciated—on the contrary; she was full-figured with more curves than the law should possibly allow. Her clothes, however, left a lot to be desired. She wore slacks, nice enough, in a navy blue color and a button-down blouse, high heels and light makeup. An outfit that didn't scream "sexy" and barely whispered "diva."

It yelled "average, nondescript, forgettable" from the business standpoint. On the personal, well, he didn't even want to think about that.

All those words were deadly in his line of work.

Then he closed his eyes, shut out the visual and simply listened to the voice bellowing from the speakers in his home studio just outside of Miami.

The throaty, rich sound of a mezzo-soprano voice filtered throughout the room. He'd listened to this demo CD more than a dozen times in twenty-four hours, had become addicted to the smooth, melodious notes. There was no doubt she had a voice, a good strong one at that, just right for singing R&B ballads and dance tunes. Ten minutes into the first listen he'd known Jason had picked a winning voice.

As for the rest, the whole package, which was what he was responsible for, that was going to be a problem.

She just didn't fit the bill. This Charlene Quinn did not look like a "diva." Hell, she didn't even look like a nightclub singer. She looked like what she was, a voice instructor at the local college. Now he did have a little more information on her, she was the daughter of a television-and-movie producer and best friends with one of the owners of Limelight Entertainment Agency. That told him two things. One, she was rich and privileged and probably thought the world was supposed to treat her exactly that way. And two, she had high connections. Limelight was a contender in the business, representing a lot of the heavy hitters in the movie as well as music industries. Still, Akil focused on the talent; connections and money meant nothing to him if his artist had no talent to work with.

On the demo she'd recorded three tracks. The first was an old Tina Turner hit, "Shake a Tail Feather," that had him bopping his head and feeling the emotional energy that up until now, only Tina had been able to infuse into her songs. The next was the song Jason heard her sing in the karaoke bar, "Hero" by Mariah Carey. Again, a tune that is probably not advised to be tried by another vocalist, but Charlene had done it amazingly well. Her vocal range was outstanding as she hit the higher notes just as easily as she rocked the lower ones.

The last tune was an unknown, the beat was slow, jazzlike, and the lyrics were sultry. More suited to the Billie Holiday and Lena Horne types. Charlene had begun with a slow steady intro that immediately caught his attention. "The first time we made love," were the lyrics and from the way she belted them out you'd think she was experiencing her first time all over again. From the verse to the chorus to the bridge, which could have been instrumentally arranged better, to the killer climax of the ballad, Akil had been transfixed, pulled into the very heart of the song and the soul of the singer.

The contradiction between her look and her sound was astounding.

Akil was a music producer and as such he was responsible for all stages of the audio development, working with the artist, studio musicians, engineers and related staff. That's what his generic duties were. But Akil hadn't risen to the spot of being one of the most sought-after producers of the decade by being generic. When he took on a new artist, he took on every aspect, from the audio to the performance to the overall image that was presented to the public. His goal was to give the listeners what they wanted, to produce the best music, to give the best images. That's what made him unique in this business, it's what made him better than most of the rest. He was known as a perfectionist, a slave driver, some had said. But in the end it was all for the best; ninety-five percent of his songs debuted in the top five on *Billboard*. Eleven of the twelve entertainers he'd been responsible for introducing to the world were top charters and now multimillionaires sought after for performances on the Grammys, the BET Awards, the MTV Awards and so on. The twelfth didn't fall into that category only because Nichelle Dante had decided after her first R&B album that she wanted to sing gospel instead. Akil had hooked her up with a great producer at Footprints Gospel Records and she was now topping the charts there.

He had an impressive record, a great reputation and money in the bank to back it up. That all started with a confidence and heartfelt belief in his artist.

Looking down into the smiling face on the picture once more, he shook his head, not sure he felt that way about Charlene Quinn.

Chapter 2

Some men went for breasts, others big booties. Akil was a thigh man, through and through. So it was no wonder that when Charlene Quinn walked into his studio, where he was seated at the mixing console, and he'd turned around in the swivel chair and was face-to-thigh with her, his pulse quickened.

He'd seen her before, her photo and in person the day they'd met at the offices of Empire Music. So he wasn't totally shocked at how pretty she actually was up close. Still, the effect of those voluptuous thighs wrapped so succulently in soft denim slacks made the rise to his feet a little slower than he'd anticipated.

A smile a mile long—no kidding, she had a beautiful, wide smile that made her eyes twinkle slightly, if one was looking at such things. Anyway, she smiled when he extended his hand and he felt the frown before he knew better to stop it.

"Ms. Quinn, I'm glad you made it safely," he said. Shaking hands was customary in business. Feeling tugs of something indescribable when his flesh touched hers was not. So he pulled away quickly and acted as if the mixing console needed more of his attention than she did.

"Ah, yes, I did get here safely. The private jet you sent helped a lot."

Her voice was deeper than he remembered, throatier, kind of like when she sang. And whatever fragrance she was wearing was playing with his senses. Luckily Akil was a big boy, he knew how to handle his urges. He also knew that urges in the direction of one of his artists was a no-no. Besides, this was Charlene Quinn, the woman who was supposed to be Playascape's next diva. He would have his hands full with this transformation without adding the sticky strings of sex to the mix.

"So, I've got a few songs from a great writer I've worked with before. I'd like you to read over them tonight, get a feel for the flow, then we'll get started first thing tomorrow morning."

He was sitting again, not really looking at her but knowing she was there.

"I thought we were having dinner tonight," she said, then cleared her throat. "I mean, Jason said I'd meet the team tonight at dinner. Doesn't that include you?"

Akil nodded. "Yes, I'll be there. But I don't want you getting it confused with a night on the town in Miami. We're here to work. I brought you out here because I can focus better in my own space. And for this CD we have a lot to focus on."

She didn't like the way he'd said that.

As a matter of fact, Charlene hadn't liked a thing about Mr. Akil Hutton since the first time she'd met him. Could anybody be as rude and arrogant as him? Probably, but she hadn't met them yet—which was saying a lot considering her background in L.A. She was finding it hard to swallow these traits from Akil.

She should have expected it, though, she'd told herself repeatedly. He was one of the most sought-after producers on the scene today. She'd been shocked when Jason told her that's who she'd be working with. Truth be told, this entire situation was still a shock to her.

While she'd always loved to sing, Charlene had never really considered a career in music. Okay, well, that wasn't exactly true. Else why would she have had a demo CD all ready when Jason asked for one? The recording had taken place more than a year ago when one of her students had written a song and asked her to sing it. When she did he'd offered to record the demo for her. But Charlene had taken those CDs and stuffed them in her dresser drawer, realizing that she'd never have the guts to send them to anyone. As much as she portrayed a strong black woman, with confidence and intelligence, Charlene knew her limitations, her weaknesses, and the main one was her appearance.

She'd never been skinny like Candis, or even petite and curvy like Rachel. That wasn't who God had meant for her to be, she accepted that. Still, some days she actually did plead with the man upstairs to just reduce her waistline by about five inches, shave off some of her thighs so she could fit in a size fourteen without busting the inner seams. As it stood, today, taking her daily supplements of Levoxyl to help increase the levels of thyroid hormones her body produced, she wore a size sixteen comfortably. And barring any flare-ups she held steady at that size.

So she hadn't pursued a singing career, hadn't wanted

people staring and gawking at her, possibly talking about her. Teaching was an ideal job because she got the chance to do what she loved and still keep a low profile. However, Rachel and Sofia had convinced her that this was an opportunity she couldn't pass up, and a small part of her knew they were right. With all her reservations, Charlene knew the smart decision was to at least give it a try. Not every singer received this chance: she'd be awfully ungrateful if she turned it down.

And now here she was, in Miami, standing in the home studio of the famous Akil Hutton wanting nothing more than to either walk out on his rude behind or sink into the floor where he couldn't notice her—both options held equal appeal at the moment.

Instead, she steeled herself, took a deep breath and pressed on. "We didn't get a chance to talk a lot about the project in L.A. I'm wondering what type of CD you have in mind."

Akil didn't even look up at her as he flicked his hand in her direction and said impatiently, "We'll get to that later. Just take the songs with you, have Nannette show you to your room and get changed for dinner."

She'd been dismissed, she was absolutely certain of that fact, and yet she still stood there. Just looking at him.

He wasn't bad on the eyes, that was also a fact. Smooth tree bark–toned skin, close-cut dark hair and clean-shaven face. He wore slacks and a long-sleeved shirt that melded around taut bicep muscles and, from what she could see, a trim stomach. His hands, she noticed as he continued to work the controls on the board, were medium-size, with long fingers, like a piano player's. He wore a gold watch but other than that no jewelry, which was outside the norm since most producers were just as jeweled-down as their artists these days.

"Is there something else?" he asked, yanking her out of her "he's damned good-looking" reverie.

"No," she said in a clipped tone. "There's nothing else. See you at dinner."

And with that she did finally turn, thanking her feet for getting the message, and stalked out of the room.

If this was any indication of how their time working together was going to be, Charlene feared this CD would never see the light of day.

The house was gorgeous, there was absolutely no doubt about that. On the ride in the limo from the airport Charlene had already assumed it would be. They'd only driven on the highway for about forty-five minutes before turning off on a road that seemed to be paved right through a forest. The stately mansion was all white with black bases around each window and a brick-colored shingled roof. It sat nestled between a scenic backdrop of even more trees. It was big and palatial, definitely a home for the enigmatic Akil Hutton.

Nervousness had swamped her as she'd stepped out of the car. The chauffeur, who'd told her at the airport his name was Cliff, had moved quickly to the trunk, unloading the two suitcases she'd brought along with her.

Now, two hours later, in the room Nannette—the pretty Latina housekeeper—had directed her to, she was standing at the window wondering what on earth she was doing. This room faced the back of the house so she had a view of the tennis courts and the corner of the pool where river rocks were piled into a small fountain.

She wasn't overwhelmed by the space. Her family home in L.A. was just about the size of this one and the homes of some of the people her family had associated with were even bigger. So it wasn't her surroundings that made her nervous. She attributed that to the man who could make or break her newfound singing career with the snap of a finger.

The low chime of her cell phone disturbed her thoughts and she moved from the window, where she'd probably been standing too long anyway, to get her purse.

"Hello?"

"Hey, Char, thanks for calling to let me know you got to Miami safely."

Sitting on the bed, Charlene used one hand to smooth down the smoke-gray skirt she planned on wearing to dinner while holding the phone in the other. "Hi, Candis. Sorry, I was sort of caught up the minute I got here."

"Really?" her older sister, with the sense of humor that skipped Charlene upon her birth, chuckled. "Caught up in what? In the arms of that fine ass Akil Hutton? I still can't believe he's going to produce your CD. You have no idea how lucky you are."

Charlene didn't even need to close her eyes to see his face again. With a little moan she said, "Girl, please. Akil Hutton isn't concerned about anything but work. Which is just fine with me because I'd just as soon get this over with."

"Get it over with? You don't sound like you're too happy about this opportunity. Which is plain crazy since you've been singing since Mama had you."

"I know, but I was happy teaching."

"No. You're happy singing."

Charlene really couldn't argue with that statement.

"But I was okay just doing it in the classroom. I don't know about performing in front of people, Candis. What will they think of me? What if they don't like my music?"

"And what if the world were struck by a nuclear bomb tomorrow? What if after I flew all the way to Paris for a photo shoot I woke up the next day with a zit the size of Texas on my forehead? What if? What if?" She sighed. "Char, you can't live your life wondering 'what if.' You've got a God-given gift, it's only right that you use it and share it with the world."

"But—"

"But nothing. Just stop worrying for a minute and go with the flow. Obviously the record execs thought enough of you to sign you to a contract and hook you up with Akil. They don't do that for just anybody."

Charlene nodded: Candis was right. The thing was, it wasn't only about talent. There were lots of talented singers out there; take the ones seen on that reality show *American Idol*. Many of the most talented singers on that show were kicked out before the final rounds. And one of the most consistent things the judges on that show—most of whom were record industry professionals in their own right—said was that it wasn't just about the voice, it was about the total package. A package Charlene wasn't so sure she had.

"I know they don't. And I'm not ungrateful for the opportunity. I'm just not a hundred percent sure about it all."

"Then it's a good thing you're not the one who has to be sure. The record execs think you're good and want to put your CD out, Akil has to think you're worth his time. So you just open your mouth and sing."

Leave it to Candis to be candid and honest with her,

almost to the point of hurting her feelings. But if there was one thing Charlene knew it was that her sister had her back. When the girls in the neighborhood—the skinny, pretty ones who came to the house to hang out with Candis—made fun of the chubby younger sister with fat, too-thick braids, Candis had rounded them all up and kicked them out. She was fiercely protective of Charlene, even though Charlene had spent most of her teenage years both envying and hating her older sister.

"You're right," she said finally, smiling because she knew on the other end of the phone Candis was probably doing the same. "I'll just do what I know how to do and pray that what's meant will be."

"What's meant is already happening," Candis said. "Now you get to work. I've got me a hot date tonight that I need to go and get ready for."

Her words reminded Charlene that Candis was on the other side of the world in Paris. "I'm sorry you're up so late checking on me. I know how you enjoy your sleep."

Candis chuckled. "You've got that right. But I had to make sure you were all right."

"I'm fine. Go ahead and get your beauty rest."

"If you didn't think to call me I know you haven't called Mama or Daddy. Give them a call when you get a minute just so they won't worry."

"I'm not you. They won't bother to worry."

"That's not true. You're their daughter just the same."

Not wanting to go into this years-old battle, Charlene cut it short. "Okay, I'll call them when I get back from dinner. You go back to sleep."

"All right. Love you, kiddo."

"Love you, too, big sis."

Clicking off the phone, Charlene knew she did love her big sister. For all that seemed different between them they were connected by a sisterly bond. As for her parents, well, that was another story entirely. But, as promised, she would call them later. After all, she was the responsible and mature sister, the one always expected to do the right thing.

She only prayed the right thing was going to dinner with Akil and the rest of the team when what she really wanted to do was teach the superproducer a thing or two about basic hospitality.

Chapter 3

Shula's Steak House wasn't exactly what Charlene had envisioned for a dinner to meet the team that would work on her CD. Something a little fancier had been her thought. But this was just as well. The dark wood floors and contemporary dining room she'd been escorted to made her feel a lot more comfortable than a dimly lit place with candles and lots of clinking crystal would have.

Not that Shula's was slacking any, no, not at all. Located in the Miami Lakes district it had topped the list on the *Miami Herald*'s Best of South Florida, easily defeating the trendy Prime 112 and Manny's Steakhouse. All places Charlene had been to in her trips to Florida and a ranking she happened to agree with.

Another surprise to her was that Akil had driven his own car to the restaurant, arriving just a few minutes after her with a tall, slim lady by his side. His bodyguards, two tall, beefy men she'd seen at the house when she was leaving, walked in looking all around the room right behind him. While her reaction to the fact that there was a gorgeous woman with Akil shouldn't have been mentionable, the momentary envy toward the woman for her small waist and long legs gave her a jolt. This wasn't new, she reminded herself. The supermodel look was more than popular where she came from and even more so in the music industry. And this woman fit the bill.

She had to be close to six feet with Akil only surpassing her height by about three or four inches. The dress she wore—or more aptly the swatch of material that covered her small, pert breasts and hugged every other inch of her from her shoulders to the upper part of her thighs, was fire-engine red and whispered sex with every step she took. Her skin was fair and coupled with her long dark hair gave her an exotic look.

Self-consciously Charlene brushed her hand over much heavier breasts and down past her thicker waist and meatier thighs. Taking slow, deep breaths, she tried not to acknowledge how much of a cliché this woman really was. She was exactly the type you'd expect to see on the arms of an NBA or NFL player, a rapper or, yes, even a superproducer like Akil.

She was so absorbed in the couple walking toward the table in the private dining room she hadn't even heard the door behind her open and close or the people who had obviously entered approach.

"Hi, Charlene. It's great seeing you again."

She turned at the touch of his hand on her shoulder and stared up happily into the smiling face of Jason Burton, the A&R rep who had first heard her sing in the karaoke bar.

"Hi, Jason. I'm glad to see you," she said with more enthusiasm than she probably should have. But it was true, she was glad to see him. Glad and hopeful that he'd be a buffer between her and Akil and his arm candy.

"Ace, my man. You made it," Jason said, standing and gripping Akil's hand in a shake.

He hadn't changed much from when she'd seen him earlier this afternoon. Well, his clothes were different. He now wore black pleated slacks and a matching jacket. The gray silk shirt that molded against his muscled chest and abs almost matched the color of her skirt. He looked cool and comfortable, yet still powerful and important. Something about the air around him, the ambience of control, made her shift uncomfortably in her seat.

After the handshake Akil reached for his date, pushing her closer to the chair where Charlene sat as if to tell her to sit there so he didn't have to. On the inside Charlene bristled but on the outside she found the strength to smile. "Good evening, Akil."

"Charlene," he said curtly, with a simple nod. "This is Serene Kravitz, head of Artist Development. Serene, meet Playascape's newest R&B artist, Charlene Quinn."

Reaching her hand up and shaking the other woman's wasn't as hard as Charlene thought it would be. Once she got over the fact that the other woman seemed to be drinking in the sight of her much like a lion would its next meal.

"Nice to meet you," Charlene said with a polite smile.

"Likewise," was Serene's response before she dropped Charlene's hand and walked around to the back of her, then to the front again. "Okay, I see what you mean, Akil. We do have our work cut out for us."

What was she talking about? The calm that Charlene had fought to obtain was quickly slipping.

"Yeah," Akil said, clearing his throat. "Let's take our seats, then we can get started."

Serene sat to one side of Charlene while Jason sat on the other. Akil sat directly across from her. They were in a private dining room so there was no one around them besides the waiters who had come out to fill their water glasses and set up buckets of ice with bottles of champagne sticking out of them.

"Where's Five and Seth?" Jason asked.

Akil shook his head, picked up a napkin and sat it in his lap. "I told them we'd see them in the morning. We don't want to overwhelm her tonight."

"But I wanted Seth to see her and maybe get an idea of her range tonight." Jason looked as perplexed as Charlene felt.

"Her voice is all right. I don't think we have to work much in that area."

Akil looked at her then, his dark eyes piercing as they found hers and held. Charlene wanted to squirm under his scrutiny, felt like slipping right out of that chair and running from that room. What was it about his glare, the intense edge to his looks, that stirred her?

"It's the other that we need to work on right away."

His words were like icicles scraping over her skin. "The other?" she asked before she could think of whether or not it was wise.

"Image and presentation, dear," Serene said, extending a long, diamond-clad hand to pat Charlene's. "That's what I do. My job is to plan your career, spearhead promotion and publicity. I create the best image for Playascape's artists and present them to the world long before the CD even hits the shelves, unlike other record labels that have downsized Artist Development to Product Development, which promotes artists heavily in the beginning of their career then stops abruptly. At Playascape we're more interested in the long-term planning."

So she wasn't *his* woman. Charlene could breathe a sigh of relief on that one. This little aspect of the business that she'd explained was new to Charlene. While she knew the ins and outs of singing and a little about recording, the workings of the back end of the music industry wasn't her forte. So Serene was like a publicist and stylist all rolled into one? Charlene had a feeling she wasn't going to like her.

"We're doing that now?" Jason asked.

"I think that's the priority," Akil responded tightly.

"The priority's always been the music."

"You know we work with the complete package at Playascape. And we don't take any shortcuts."

Suddenly she could see exactly what Akil meant. The "big picture" was her. Her appearance, to be specific. He didn't seem worried about her voice because he'd already heard that, no doubt. What he was worried about was her look. Did she look like the singing stars hogging the charts these days? To that the answer was a resounding no.

Glancing down at her gray pencil skirt and white blouse, cinched at the waist with a thick black patent leather belt, she didn't see Beyoncé's tightly honed curves and blatant sex appeal. Lifting a hand to her thick hair lying on her shoulders in heavy curls didn't bring to mind the short, sexy cuts of Rihanna or Keri Hilson. She just wasn't in the same class as those acts. But she could sing. That was not a question.

"I see what he's saying, Jason. We have to make sure

every aspect of this CD is top-notch. Not just the vocals but everything that comes before and after the listener hears the music. Is that right, Akil?"

His gut clenched the moment he heard his name on her lips. She was looking right at him, one smoothly arched brow lifting over her hazel eyes.

He'd been trying to keep his composure. And to do that he found he needed to look at her directly as infrequently as possible. From her picture he'd thought she was pretty. Earlier today in the studio he'd felt a powerful thrust of lust at being so close to her voluptuous frame. Now, tonight, when he was supposed to be on his A game as her producer, he found it almost impossible to avoid the subtle hints of sexuality pouring from her.

Did she know what she was doing to him? Did she have any idea how the moment she'd touched her hand to her chest, smoothed down her clothes to her thighs, he'd wanted to clear the room of everybody but the two of them? When her fingers had grazed her hair he'd sighed inwardly, wondering how the soft strands would feel between his fingers. And her scent, it wafted through the air covering even the mouthwatering aroma of perfectly seasoned and cooked steaks throughout the restaurant.

No, he answered himself as he found the courage to look into her eyes once more. She didn't know. Had no idea how she was turning him on. He'd know if she did because there'd be some semblance of triumph that she was getting to him. Akil had seen it a million times with groupies and other industry females. Charlene didn't have that, the look of a hunter, he'd called it. And that angered him just a little more because that meant she didn't easily fit into any mold.

"That's correct. Listeners today are much more

interested in the personal lives and the looks of an artist than they've ever been before. Twenty years ago the R&B reins were held by such heavy hitters as Whitney Houston and Anita Baker, where voices carried you to another plateau. Today's listeners are much more materialistic. Everybody wants the bling, the high life, but most can only get it living vicariously through entertainers," Akil affirmed.

"That's why Beyoncé's bootylicious persona sells records," Charlene added.

"And once we get you into shape, yours will, too," Serene said with a smile. "I think I'll have Carlo come down for a look-see, Akil. You know he can work wonders with anybody. She may have to go to the spa for a week or so. I'd like to introduce her to the public at the Vibe Awards in two months."

"No!" Akil said so loudly Charlene jumped.

"Man, what's up with you tonight?" Jason asked. "First you say appearance is priority now you're axing Serene's plan."

He shook his head, unable to keep his thoughts straight. But he knew what Serene was saying, knew what she was thinking as far as Charlene went, and had to put a stop to it. Sure, he'd thought the same thing initially, but that was before Charlene had arrived in Miami. Before she'd stood close enough for him to smell her or looked so enticing he could imagine tasting her.

"That's not what I have in mind," he said finally, motioning for the waiter to come over and open the bottle of champagne. "I want her polished and ready to go at Vibe." He took a sip of his bubbly and managed to look at Charlene again. He'd thought about her all afternoon but wasn't entirely sure of this new direction until this very moment. "But I don't want her dieting down to a size two. I think the best way to present her is to be different. To take R&B back to its roots."

To his surprise, Charlene lifted her glass to the waiter, watched as the chilled liquid filled to the top then licked her lips before taking a sip. "You mean you're going to let me sing like Tina Turner and Gladys Knight did and not worry about the highly commercialized packages gracing the airwaves today?"

Akil nodded, inwardly applauding her intelligence. He had a feeling that there was much more to Charlene Quinn then he'd originally thought.

"That's exactly what we're going to do."

Chapter 4

Music soothed his soul. Always had and Akil suspected always would.

Sitting back in the chair, pushing the springs as far as they would go, he folded his hands behind his head and stared up at the ceiling. He was in his Miami home, past the personal rooms to the back where his studio was located. In the background a slow beat played. The piano solo was coming up in a few minutes, after the tight strain of violin notes. It was a riveting beat, an emotional ballad that he'd composed but had yet to find the words to accompany.

Be better than me, Akil. Promise me you'll be better.

The familiar words echoed in his mind. That's where they lived now, twelve years later. They were a whisper on swollen and ashen lips, a plea from the one person he'd loved the most at the time.

He'd made the promise. And he'd kept it. He was better than her. His life, because of hers, had gone down a similar path with an entirely different mind-set, one that brought him fame and fortune, everything he'd ever wished for.

But also one that had cost him much.

It was times like these, times when it was quiet except for the music of his heart, that he thought of his past, of the life he had left behind.

Of the one person he'd wanted so desperately to help but who was completely unreachable to him.

"Akil."

At the sound of his name he was jolted out of the past.

"I'm sorry. I didn't mean to disturb you," Charlene was saying, already backing out of the room.

"No," he said, halting her instantly with the single word. "It's okay. Stay."

She'd changed into lounge pants and a T-shirt that brushed just above her knees. On her feet she wore slippers and on her face a look of confusion that scraped over his already tense nerves. How did she do that? How did she look so naive and so innocent one minute, then open her mouth to talk and sound older and much wiser than he could ever be the next?

"I went to the kitchen for some water and heard the music."

"I'm sorry. I should have closed the outer doors to block out the sound. I didn't mean to wake you."

She was shaking her head, the long hair she'd pulled up into a ponytail swaying behind her.

"You didn't wake me. I can never sleep the first night I'm away from home." She was shrugging the words off as if she were embarrassed by them. "This is nice. Did you write it?" she asked about the music.

He nodded.

"What's it called?"

"Nothing right now. The music was in my head one day so I composed it. But I haven't come up with the words or theme for it yet."

It was her turn to nod as if she understood exactly what he was saying. "It's kind of sad," she commented.

Pushing the button, he looped the song, let the slow, heated beginning start.

"Kind of."

They remained quiet, letting the music move around them.

"But kind of inspiring, encouraging."

Leaning forward, he rested his elbows on his knees. "She's growing. Learning."

"She?"

"I always call songs 'she.' Females have a lot more emotion, empathy, compassion, triumph, in their souls than men."

She smiled. "You think so, huh? I guess I can relate to that."

"Being a female, I figured you could."

After a few more beats she said, "He's giving her something."

"Something that moves her to another level."

"It moves them both. See right here," she said, lifting a finger in the air just as the piano solo picked up the beat and drowned out the keyboard and percussions. "Right here is where it changes from just her song to their song. To their journey."

For a moment he was quiet, letting her words and

the music sink in. "You're right," he said finally, almost incredulously. "You have a good ear."

"I studied instrumental composition in college."

He sat back, let his eyes gaze at her once more. Each time he looked at her he could swear he saw something else. This time she looked vulnerable, yet capable. Weak only in that she was new to this scenery, but strong in that she was determined to make the best of her situation. He admired that.

And in that instant he feared her.

"You should get some rest. We're starting early tomorrow and will probably work all day. Did you look at the songs I gave you?" Turning his attention back to the board, he cut off the music and began shutting down the rest of the power.

She hesitated and Akil almost turned to see if she was still there. But then she answered him in a voice just a tad smaller, a hint less enthusiastic than it had been a moment before.

"I'll be ready for tomorrow's session. You don't have to worry, Akil. I teach my students how to sing and probably know just as much about vocals, if not more, than you do. So I won't let you down."

Before he had a chance to say that wasn't what he meant, that he'd just wanted to make sure she was prepared, she was gone.

Cursing, Akil slammed his palms down on the mixing console, standing and pushing the chair away from him so hard it slammed into the wall a few feet away. "Dammit!" he cursed, then flicked the light off and left the studio himself.

Why did it always seem like he said the wrong thing to her?

* * *

Felix "Five Minute" Hernendez was one of the best sound technicians in the business. He'd also been known for the number-one hit he'd written for Lady X two years ago in about five minutes, hence his nickname.

Seth Dante was the sound engineer. Charlene knew because Jason had told her all about Seth and Five last night during dinner. Right about the time Serene had been giving Akil scathing looks because of the direction he wanted to take with her image. It was comforting to know now that Akil had plans to work her career around the real her.

There was a guitar player whom she hadn't been introduced to yet but could see was already set up and touching the strings on his guitar in the soundproof isolation booth. She'd figured the music had already been digitally recorded by using a gobo panel to keep the sound from bleeding into the other microphones as she sang. But, of course, Akil knew what he was doing. She was sure he had as much control of each instrument channel at the mixing board as he planned to have of her and her voice.

This is it, Charlene told herself, standing in the doorway of the studio. She must have spent the better part of four or five hours reading over the songs Akil had given her, practically memorizing the musical arrangements, the high notes, the lows, the climax of each song. And she was ready, she knew she was ready.

With her bottled water in hand, she moved into the studio full of people, taking a deep breath before saying, "Good morning."

All eyes immediately turned to her and a small nip of fear touched her. Stamping it down, she smiled even brighter and walked right between the huddled group of men.

"Good morning, sunshine," Jason said in his always playful voice. Leaning forward, he kissed her on the cheek. "Somebody call the police. It has got to be a crime for someone to be as beautiful as you are this early in the morning."

Charlene chuckled. "One, eleven o'clock is not that early. And two, that was one weak-ass line."

Jason laughed right along with her. "Yeah, you're right. You're right. C'mon, let's get started."

A tall guy with spiked raven-black hair and a touch of gold in front of his mouth reached out a bony arm toward her. He was dressed in jeans and a Pittsburgh Steelers jersey and she couldn't help but smile. "If I'd known we were showing our teams I would have worn my Raiders shirt," she said.

His smile spread and she was thankful to see there was really only one gold tooth in his mouth and not a row full like some of the acts in the industry these days. Still, he looked young enough to be one of her students.

"You got jokes," he said. "You're on the East Coast now. You can't come in here with that West Coast nonsense."

"Whatever," she said, letting him clasp her hand.

"I'm Five," he introduced himself.

Charlene liked him instantly and knew they were going to work well together.

"And I'm Seth. And that's T-Rock on the bass. He's going to be in the booth with you because his sound is crisper in there."

A shorter man with caramel-toned skin and green eyes stepped up to her then, pointing to the tall

Caucasian guitarist she'd already noted in the isolation booth. She was about to take his offered hand when Akil interrupted.

"If you're all finished gaping over her like you've never seen a female before, we can get started."

His voice was like a blast of arctic air, chilling the room instantly and snapping her spine straight.

"Let's start with 'Never Before Like This.'" He continued to bark orders and she watched as Five took his place, moving into the control room with Akil.

Seth went to stand near the DAW, the digital audio workstation, which usually took the place of mixing consoles, recorders, synthesizers, samplers and sound-effects devices. She noted Akil still had a mixing console that he liked to control on his own. Seth was probably the backup he needed to complete the full sound. Meanwhile, Jason walked her over to the booth and attempted to help her with the headphones.

"She knows how to do it, Jase," Akil snapped. "Come on, we've got a lot to get done."

He was in his desired spot in the control room with what she could see was his game face on. He was all about business today. Whereas last night when she'd seen him in that very same position he'd looked, for just that short amount of time, human.

"I've got it, Jason. Thanks." Picking up the headphones, she moved to the stand, dropped her music down onto it and took her place in front of the mic.

She liked this song a lot. Its tempo began slowly but then picked up with the verse. It was good old-fashioned R&B, just what she loved to sing. So if Mr. Superproducer was all about business this morning then she could be, too. She was going to sing this song and every other song he put in front of her like her very life depended on it. Because Akil Hutton was not going to beat her. Not here, not today.

"Never like this before. No, never like this. I never loved like this. Never kissed like this. Never felt like this before."

This was the fifth time she'd sung this song, the fifth time he'd listened to her take the verse written on that song sheet apart only to put it back together in her own special way again.

Her voice rocketed through the air, tore through the speakers and rubbed along the contours of his heart. It was strong, practiced, professional. She hit every note and then hit it again even better the next time around. His palms had begun to sweat, his pulse quickening with the music.

They'd been at it for hours, stopped for about forty-five minutes for lunch, and went at it some more. She never faltered. He'd worked with a lot of artists in his time, had seen a lot of commercial acts. Females who could sing well enough in their church choir or in a talent contest and looked hotter than a house full of strippers. But they weren't serious. He'd known it then, but he'd worked his magic, got enough recorded to make their CD one of the hottest out there. All the while knowing, deep down inside, they weren't real singers. They didn't have real talent. Sure, they were commercial and they were still selling lots of records, selling out concerts and making him and Playascape a boatload of money.

But at the end of the day, at night when he lay down to sleep, he felt like a sellout.

He wasn't producing music anymore, he was making money. But now, listening to Charlene Quinn, he felt that old surge inside, that old feeling when he listened to such greats as Aretha and Ella, Gladys and Dionne. He felt like Charlene could be the one.

"Let's do it again and tape it this time. Get it right and you're done for the night. We can remix after you're gone."

He knew his tone was clipped, cold, distant. But that's what it had to be. The way he needed it to stay. Or he'd lose more than just the chance to work with this new talent—he'd lose himself.

Chapter 5

"Okay, tell me what's going on?" Jason asked Akil the moment they were alone in the sound booth. Seth and Five were working on remixing the track they'd just finished with Charlene in the live room and Serene had gone home for the day. Serene made some remark about getting Carlo here as soon as possible and Akil had made sure to correct her, just as he had last night.

"No dieting. I want what she's already got spruced up, build her image from there. Got it?"

No, Serene didn't get it and neither did he, that's why Jason was questioning his partner and longtime friend now.

"What? We're making this CD. What do you think is going on?"

"I think you've got something else on your mind than this music, something that might interfere with us getting this CD done."

"C'mon, Jason. You know me better than that. Nothing interferes with my music."

Jason folded his arms over his chest and leaned against the wall. "Tell me what you have in mind for her."

Akil didn't answer as quickly as he normally would have. Another fact that concerned Jason.

"Like I said last night, I think we should go old-school with her. Back to the roots of R&B and steer clear of the commercial BS."

Jason nodded. "The commercial BS is what's made us rich over the last ten years."

"I don't deny that."

"It's built our reputation, made this label a number-one contender with anything Sony, Arista, Columbia or the rest of them have. We're the hottest thing in the game right now. Why would you want to mess with that?"

Akil sighed, sat back in his chair and glared at Jason. "Because I'm tired of it. I'm tired of putting out average CDs and calling it music. Tired of the gimmicky groups and half-assed singers we reform and glamorize then slap a label on them and put them on the shelves. I want to make real music, to listen to the real sound of R&B again. Can you relate to that?"

Jason had to pause a moment at the words and the amount of money they stood to lose if this didn't work. "You're serious?"

"As a heart attack after years of fast-food burgers." He ran a hand over his face. "I think Charlene's got real talent, Jase. I think she has longevity to make it in this business. But I also think that Playascape needs something fresh, something different. I don't want us to be typecast, putting out the same product year after year. I want us to grow."

Jason nodded. "I see what you're saying. And I hear you about Charlene, she's not like the others we've worked with. But you know Empire's got a lot of money invested in this. I don't know that going against the grain right at this moment is financially feasible for us."

"It is," Akil said adamantly. "Empire's been distributing us for years. They know we're perfectionists and that we bring the money to the table when it counts. They trust us. The question is, do you trust me?"

It was a moment of truth, one of those times when friendship had to be the glue to hold things together. Jason had doubts but they were minimal compared to all the times Akil had come through. Just like he'd trusted his gut when he first heard Charlene sing and rushed to get her signed, he trusted that Akil's vision was going to work. That they were going to make Charlene a success, a different kind of success.

"Yeah, man. You know I trust you," Jason said finally, reaching out to shake Akil's hand.

Akil stood, shaking Jason's hand then pulling him in for a hug. "It's going to be big. The biggest thing we've ever done, Jase. Watch and see."

He picked up the phone again. Alone in his bedroom in the wee hours of the morning, Akil knew he should be asleep, gearing up for tomorrow's session. But he couldn't rest.

Charlene's powerful voice had brought back memories. Some painful and some happy—some that just need to be addressed once and for all.

Dialing the number, he sat back on his bed, leaning forward so that his elbows rested against his knees. Looking down to the floor as he held the phone to his ear waiting for the call to connect, he wiggled his toes in the ultra-soft dark blue carpet. It lined the entire length of his master suite until it opened up to the deck, which was tiled with black marble speckled with a blue similar to the carpet. His walls were painted a subtle gray, his furniture, sparse, sleek and expensive. The entertainment center that spanned the entire left wall was state-of-the-art with Dolby sound and a sixty-inch mounted plasma. Music was his life and so it surrounded him wherever he went. Even in his bathroom there was a sound system, designed to match the black-and-blue color scheme in there, as well.

He'd arrived, he thought as the overseas connection had finally been made and the line rang in his ear. He'd arrived at rich and famous, just as he'd always planned. And he liked it here, or so he thought.

His childhood hadn't been easy and neither had hers. But he'd made them both a promise, to get them out and to make them both happy. He succeeded in one area and drastically failed in the other.

She hated him, had told him as much more times than he could count. Yet, he still loved her, still held a place for her in his heart.

Charlene reminded him of that place. She reminded him of Lauren.

"Centro di riabilitazione del Seminary di buona mattina," a female voice answered speaking quick Italian that Akil struggled to understand.

"Ah, *buona mattina,*" he said, clearing his throat and sitting up straight as if the person on the other end of the phone could see him. "Lauren Jackson, please?"

He hated that name, hated the way it rolled off his tongue with complete bitterness and contempt.

"Chi è questo?"

"Akil Hutton."

The line went quiet and he waited, heart pounding against his chest, palms sweating. He hadn't spoken to her in more than three years. Not necessarily all his fault. He'd written to her a couple of times but had only recently found a number where she could be reached.

"Ms. Jackson non è disponibile. Non denomini ancora," she said and hung up without another word.

From traveling all over the world on business Akil had picked up a basic understanding of most languages like Italian, French, hell, he even knew a little German because one of his artists was a big hit in Germany. From the woman's clipped words he gathered two things: (1) that Lauren was definitely a patient at the Seminary Rehabilitation Hospital and (2) that she did not want to speak to him. The words *not available* and the stern *do not call again* sort of tipped him off.

Lauren was in Milan and she was in a rehab center. That meant she was safe and she was getting the help she so desperately needed. That should have been enough for him.

And he shouldn't still be plagued with guilt. Yet he was and there was nothing he could do about it.

Chapter 6

"So how's it going?" Rachel asked the moment Charlene answered her cell phone at a little after ten the next morning.

"It's going," she replied, falling back onto the bed. She'd already showered and was dressed. They were starting at ten-thirty this morning and every other morning unless Akil said otherwise, that's what Jason had told her yesterday. She'd had another restless night, unable to get the contrary man and his beguiling eyes out of her mind. But with the rising of the sun she'd tried to shield herself from that negativity, embracing the new day ahead. Hopefully it would work.

"Uh-oh, that doesn't sound good."

Rachel knew her too well, just as well as Candis did, and that was too well for both of them, Charlene thought suddenly.

"What's going on? You don't like the songs? You

know, if you call Sofia she can pull some strings, maybe get you another producer or something."

"No, it's not that. I just mean that we got right down to business. Akil's every bit as focused as we'd heard. I got a firsthand look at how much of a perfectionist he really is."

"Again, that doesn't sound good. You don't like him?"

Afraid that the answer to that question was the real problem, Charlene closed her eyes and took a deep breath. "I didn't say that. He's just different."

"Okay," Rachel said, exaggerating the word. "So he's different from all the other superproducers who wanted to work with you on your debut CD?"

"No. I didn't say it like that. You know I'm grateful for this opportunity. Hell, I wouldn't even be in this position without your pushing me up onto that stage."

Rachel chuckled. "Now why doesn't that sound grateful to me?"

"I am grateful, really. Jeez, you and Candis are really ganging up on me this week."

"You talked to Candis? Where is she this week?"

"Paris."

"Lucky girl."

"You're sort of lucky yourself with that hunky actor you've got feelin' you," Charlene countered.

"I so do not want to talk about Ethan right now. This call is about you and how you're making out. I think I might need to fly out there."

Charlene was shaking her head as she sat straight up on the bed. She knew that Rachel was in Hollywood on the set of *Paging the Doctor,* where she was makeup artist and wardrobe designer. The show was in its final weeks of taping for the season but Rachel had already taken a two-week hiatus when the story of her affair with Ethan Chambers had hit the press. She was almost positive her friend couldn't just hop on a plane and come to Miami. But that wasn't saying much. When Rachel put her mind to doing something there was usually no stopping her.

"You definitely do not need to do that. I'm fine. The situation is fine. I don't need you or Sofia getting involved."

"Good, because Sofia's got enough on her plate. I swear, if that girl doesn't slow down and start to enjoy life I don't know what's going to happen to her."

Sofia was Rachel's older sister and Charlene's agent. She'd known Sofia for as long as she'd known Rachel, but since Sofia was older by nine years they'd rarely hung out together. But the moment Rachel heard of Jason's interest she'd volunteered Sofia as her agent. Sofia hadn't minded at all; she loved her job as an entertainment agent and was waiting for the day she could take full charge of Limelight Entertainment. At the moment she was second in charge to Jacob Wellesley, the uncle that raised her and Sofia after their parents' untimely deaths.

"She's still working twenty-five hours a day, eight days a week." That was a joke between her and Rachel. Sofia worked so much they'd started to believe that there were extra hours and days created just for her hectic schedule.

"Is she? I'm almost ready to run in that house and tie her to the bed for a full month."

They both chuckled but Charlene could hear the concern in Rachel's voice. She knew her friend was really worried about her sister. For that matter, so was she. Besides being her agent, Sofia was just like family to Charlene. "Let's pray she comes to her senses soon. I definitely don't want to see you and her going at it as you try to tie her down."

"You know you're coming along for backup so don't even try to get out of it."

Again Charlene found herself laughing, which was a good thing. She needed to be in as positive a mood as possible to deal with Akil today. Oh, dang it, Akil!

"Girl, I am so late. I've gotta get going. Akil's going to have a fit."

"Damn, he's clocking you?"

"Not like that. You know this is a job. I was supposed to be in the studio at ten-thirty. Talking to you, it's now ten minutes to eleven."

Rachel was laughing. "Okay, go on. But I really don't think he's going to dock your pay."

"It's about professionalism, Rachel."

"Girl, you don't have to tell me. You know I live by those same rules. Tell Akil it was my fault and apologize profusely on my behalf. If that doesn't work then maybe I really will have to fly out there."

"No, you stay right where you are. I'll handle Mr. Akil just fine on my own."

Clicking off the call and tossing the phone on the bed, Charlene made a hasty retreat out of the room hoping she really could handle Akil, the superproducer with his manic mood swings, on her own.

"Do you need a personal wake-up call, Ms. Quinn?" was the first thing Akil said to her.

A hot retort simmered at the back of her throat just itching to be released. However, she *was* late. And she'd anticipated his reaction all the way down the steps and the long foyer that took her to the west end of the house where the studio was located. He had reason to be angry, she knew, so she'd suck up her own attitude at his tart words and take it. "I apologize. I was on a call and—"

He held up a hand to halt her words. "You will learn in this industry that time is money. And it's usually somebody else's money. So make this the last late appearance and we'll remain on a good note."

What? Had they ever been on a good note?

Charlene only shook her head, bypassed the live room and headed straight for the isolation booth. She wasn't sure what song they were working on this morning but it didn't matter, she'd read over the song sheets so many times she probably knew all of them by heart. Stepping inside the booth, she noted she was alone today. The music tracks had apparently already been laid for whatever they were working on.

"Since you were wasting your voice talking on the phone, let's go through some warm-ups," Akil said through the speakers in the room.

Casting a quick glance toward the live room, she tried not to frown or show that he was getting on her nerves. A fact that only aggravated the new conflict roiling through her. Despite all his negative traits she thought Akil Hutton was attractive. There, she'd admitted it to herself finally. Even now she found herself honing in on the dark tint of his skin, the rich brown color of his eyes. Eyes that held her captive each time she dared look at them.

"You do know about vocal exercises, I presume."

She did. She taught them to her students every day. Taking a deep breath, she vowed to bite her traitorous tongue and squelch what she hoped was a minor attraction—or temporary bout of insanity.

She simply nodded in his direction, attempted a stiff

smile, then straightened her posture. Steady and sure of herself, she began to breathe. Slowly she inhaled and exhaled using her diaphragm, making sure she wasn't forcing any air. This was a common error with novice singers, forcing their voice by breathing incorrectly. An experienced singer did not need to force their voice to produce a good strong sound; that caused too much pressure against the cords and could damage the voice permanently.

She was in full work mood and nothing, not even the fine temperamental producer, was going to stop her.

She is perfect, Akil thought with alarm.

A perfectly trained singer, he amended but still didn't feel that was quite adequate.

Even now as he watched her he felt there was something else—something more to her that seemed to touch him. That touch was both alarming and unwanted, new and familiar in a way that again scared him. Akil wasn't afraid of anything. He'd grown up on the drug-infested streets of east Baltimore and didn't flinch at the sight or thought of death. How could he when it was an everyday possibility where he'd lived? Those streets had made him the man he was today—the one who wasn't afraid to take risks, to reach for what he wanted then hold on tight when he got it. Nothing tripped him up, nothing made him think twice about his goals, his aspirations. For as long as he could remember it had been that way, for better or for worse.

Until now.

Until Charlene.

He had realized that the moment she began to sing yesterday. She'd rehearsed the song, that was the first thing that surprised him. For a woman who had buried herself in a school, surrounded herself with aspiring singers but hadn't chased the dream for herself, she was surprisingly professional and on cue.

She'd known the exact pitches to hit, even though this was her first time singing the song with music. Normally he had to rehearse a song with an artist for at least a day before they could begin recording anything, but at midnight last night he and Jason were remixing her voice over the music, blending the two together until they almost had a perfect recording.

Her talent was amazing and Akil wished his attraction to her stopped there.

Unfortunately for him, the rest of Charlene Quinn was even harder to resist. From her infectious smile that reminded him of the few happier moments in his life to the fire he saw in her eyes when she sang, she was gorgeous. And while she seemed completely oblivious to it, she was sexy as hell. Take right now, for instance; here they were in the studio supposedly working. He'd given her the simple task of vocal warm-ups. He'd assumed this would be painless; of course a vocal teacher could do vocal warm-ups. He'd really just wanted to get her reaction to the order. Wanted to see if she would tell him she didn't need to warm up, that she knew what she was doing. Instead she'd just done what he'd asked and now he was paying the price.

His gaze was locked on her lips as she sang the scale up and then back down again.

Her voice rose when needed, dipped when expected, flawlessly working the scale in a way he'd rarely seen or heard done.

Her lips were a little shiny, both from the gloss he noted she'd worn when she came in and from the water she'd sipped just before starting the warm-ups. They looked soft and warm and he couldn't help but wonder how they'd taste.

At her waist her arms lifted until one hand centered on her belly. Her back was straight and he watched the rise and fall of her breasts as she sang. *Voluptuous* wasn't exactly the right word for Charlene's body— *mouthwatering* described it much better in his mind. Her jeans were fitting thighs he'd watched for the last two days and imagined were as soft as her mouth. The shirt she wore today wasn't formfitting—a fact he had noted with most of her clothes—yet the soft fabric draped over the curve of her breasts in a way that had him growing hard the moment she had entered the studio. That was most likely the reason he'd snapped at her.

Maybe if this were a different time or if he were at a different place in his life, wanting her physically wouldn't bother him so much. But he wasn't. Lately, memories had been haunting him, a sense of dread that he hadn't felt since he was a teenager looking over his shoulder on the dark city streets crept down his spine. Something was about to happen, he just had no idea what.

Ms. Charlene Quinn might be that something.

Chapter 7

Twelve hours. That's how long they'd been in the studio. Today's session moved a lot more slowly than yesterday's. Charlene attributed that to the surly attitude of her star producer.

On the one hand, she couldn't dismiss Akil's talent or his keen sense of knowing what worked and what didn't. On the other, his personality sucked!

All day she'd been singing, taking his direction and starting over and over again. This song, "Break You Down," had a dance rhythm, it was fast and sexy and hip. There was even a rap part that Jason said they were trying to get Young Jeezy, Drake or Ludacris to do. Her personal preference would have been Ludacris but from the way Akil looked at Jason when he'd told her this, she figured she'd best keep that opinion to herself.

Now it was just past midnight, she was tired and hungry and cranky.

"Okay, let's try this—" Akil began saying.

But Jason, who had just come into the isolation booth with her to see how she was doing, pushed the intercom button and interrupted him.

"I think it's a wrap for today, Akil. She needs to get some rest."

Akil's frown was instant, his dark gaze seeking hers. And her eyes found his just like she knew they would. It was as if she knew the exact moment he was going to look at her, like they were drawn together like magnets. It was eerie and stirring all at the same time.

She didn't open her mouth although she desperately wanted to agree with Jason. Instead she waited for Akil's response. But he didn't say a thing, only continued to stare at her as if she were the only person in the room.

"Fine," was his tight reply.

She released the breath she hadn't been aware she was holding the moment he looked away from her.

"Listen, I'm sorry about that. I don't know what's going on with him. He's usually not this bad."

Charlene had already slipped off the stool she'd been sitting on and stretched. "You mean he's not always a mean SOB?"

Jason chuckled. "Yeah, that's exactly what I mean. He's a perfectionist and he gets the job done. I just don't know what's up with the attitude lately."

She nodded. "Maybe it's just me," she said, absently moving toward the door to let them both out.

"You know, I think you're right."

Stopping abruptly at his words, she turned to face him and asked, "Really? You think I did something to piss him off?"

"Oh, no," he replied quickly. "Nothing like that. You're doing a great job. I mean, I've worked with a lot of singers and you've got them beat by a long shot. Don't worry about it," he said, putting an arm around her and walking toward the main door of the studio.

"Okay, well, I'm off to bed. I'll see you two in the morning," she said, deciding quickly that Akil Hutton's bad attitude was taking too much of her energy for one day. But just as she was nearing the door, now a few feet away from Jason, Akil stepped out of the live room.

"You know this is serious business, Charlene. If you can't hang, just let me know."

The professional in her said to smile, say good-night and keep going, but the other part of her, the one that lived by the motto I Am Woman, Hear Me Roar, spun around so quickly she could have snapped her neck.

"I understand this is serious business, Mr. Hutton. I'm doing my job. If you have a problem with it, just let me know."

Folding his arms over his chest only made him look angrier—not intimidating the way she figured he'd meant.

"My problem is with your carefree attitude. Despite the impression others may have given," he said, cutting an evil eye at Jason, "we don't play all day. This is about working hard to achieve a finished product we're all happy with. A CD that will sell. A product we can market."

Her hand was sliding to her hip before she could stop it and she'd taken a step closer to Akil. "And you don't think I want the same thing?"

"I don't think you know how serious this all is."

"I flew down here, didn't I? I studied the songs like you told me. I sang for eleven hours yesterday and almost twelve and a half today. I did the warm-ups you requested although you and I both know it was unnecessary. I've adhered to all the changes you've made in the song when again, we both know, they weren't necessary. What else would you have me do to show I'm serious about this business, as you call it? Jump through hoops singing nursery rhymes backward?"

Jason stuffed his hands into his pockets, looking like he didn't know what to say to either of them. And Akil just stood there. Not saying anything and not budging.

"Good night, Charlene," was all he finally managed.

Biting back the rest of what she wanted to say to him she looked directly at Jason. "Good night, Jason."

He was an idiot.

Ten times an idiot, he'd told himself with each step he took upstairs.

"You're trippin'," was all Jason had said to him the moment Charlene left them alone. Akil had to admit his longtime friend was absolutely right.

He was trippin'. Over the fact that Charlene reminded him of Lauren and over the fact that he was attracted to her. This was not how he usually handled women and it was certainly not how he handled clients. What the hell was wrong with him?

Akil didn't have a clear answer to that question, but had decided to put an end to at least one of his mistakes. He'd been wrong to treat Charlene the way he did and Akil always admitted when he was wrong.

Just apologize and say good-night, he told himself when he finally stood in front of her door. *Tomorrow's a fresh start,* he recited in his mind while lifting a hand and knocking softly.

It seemed like an eternity standing there in the hallway, his fingers clenching and unclenching at his sides. He was about to give up, figuring she was already asleep and turning to leave, when she opened the door.

"Akil?" Even the sound of his name in her voice was alluring. He was so busted. "Did you have something else to say to me?" she asked in a frostier tone.

He deserved it.

"Yes, I did." Taking a deep breath, he looked right into her eyes. No, more like fell into the complete compassion and honesty he saw there. Damn, could he feel like more of a fool?

"Look, I apologize for acting like an ass today."

She raised one of those thick, arched eyebrows and he sighed.

"Okay, I apologize for acting like an ass since you've arrived. I've been rude and harsh and it was totally uncalled for."

She nodded her head slowly and his gaze slipped from her eyes to what she was wearing.

"I accept your apology," she said, taking a step back like she was retreating into the room to leave him standing out there.

But that was a no-no.

In the time it had taken him to curse himself, shut down the studio and walk upstairs, she'd changed from the jeans and shirt she was wearing to a floor-length nightgown. It shouldn't have been sexy because it showed nothing but her bare arms. Every other inch of her was covered all the way up to the shoelace-type tie at the base of her neck. Whatever, it made her butter-toned skin appear even more radiant, her eyes just a tad exotic.

He felt himself stiffen as his eyes raked over her, up and down and down and up. The moment she moved he reached for her, grabbed her by the elbow and took a step closer so that they were face-to-face.

She opened her mouth to speak and he knew there would be an argument. She'd tell him to get off of her and he'd refuse, it would go nowhere. So instead he simply lowered his head, let his lips touch hers lightly and shivered at the connection.

Releasing her arm and pretty certain that she wasn't going to run, Akil lifted both hands and cupped her perfect face, tilting her mouth so that it was easier for his taking. He'd meant to move slow, to sort of sip on her sweetness, but the moment his tongue touched hers, slow and sweet withered away.

Instead the kiss turned into a firestorm, bolts of lightning probably fizzled above them as he moved closer, sank deeper into her taste. Somewhere in the distance he thought he heard her moan, then her palms flattened on his chest. Something feral and distinct rose in his chest and he took more and more.

She sighed. Or was it him?

Her hands slipped downward, wrapped around his waist.

He moaned, but then again, it could have been her.

His thumbs brushed over her cheekbones as his teeth bit lightly on her bottom lip.

"Damn."

Somebody said it, he just didn't know who.

Her tongue traced his top lip and he shook, right down to his toes, his entire body vibrated. He took her lower lip, suckled for a moment before diving back into the warmth of her mouth. It was fevered and hurried, urgent and dire. He wanted so much more, needed this to last just a little bit longer.

At the same time warning bells echoed in his head,

chiming and all but chanting for him to stop, to take this slow, to be sure. He pulled back, tore his lips from hers, but couldn't bear to stop touching her. Breathing like he'd just run a marathon, he rested his forehead on hers, felt her trying to steady herself, as well.

"I didn't do that because I like you," he said gruffly, his hand still cupping her face.

"Then you must lie as good as you produce music," she replied, pulling out of his embrace, stepping back into her room and closing the door quietly.

Chapter 8

Akil Hutton liked her.

The superproducer with the volatile dark brown eyes, multimillion-dollar bank account and cranky attitude liked her. The not-so-skinny woman who loved to sing but didn't want the spotlight.

Rolling over in the king-size bed with mauve satin sheets in a room she'd only been in for three days but already felt comfortable in, Charlene smothered a smile with the back of her hand.

He'd come to apologize and she'd accepted. She hadn't a moment to digest that little bit of information before he was in her face, touching her arm, his lips moving against hers.

It had been strange to kiss him. To kiss Akil.

She'd kissed men before, no way was she inexperienced in that area. She'd kissed men and had sex.

Yet the three experiences she'd had were just a reaction to the attraction of male and female.

Clutching a pillow in her arms, she relaxed to the notion that she was attracted to Akil. Hadn't she already accepted that fact yesterday? Yeah, but that was before he'd been, in his own words, "an ass" after their recording session.

And before he'd kissed her.

As she lifted a hand back to her mouth, one finger slid slowly over lips that still tingled from his touch. Hours later it felt like he'd just pulled away, just stopped giving her the best kiss she'd ever had.

Then he'd pulled away and said something else stupid. She'd swear that man invented the concept of not knowing what to say out of his mouth. Sitting up in the bed abruptly, she craned her neck to look at the clock on the nightstand. The last thing she wanted was to be late for another session. Only Akil hadn't said what time today's session was going to start. *Forget it,* she thought, moving her legs and letting her feet hit the floor. She'd be early if that were the case.

Twenty minutes later, after her shower and slipping into a turquoise-and-white sundress that hugged her breasts, tied around the neck and hung loose to her ankles, she moved to the closet and surveyed herself in the floor-length mirror. She loved this dress because besides the curve of her breasts that were lifted high in her super-supportive bustier, no other aspect of her figure was decipherable. She'd fussed for a few minutes with her hair, adding some curl to the normally plain ponytail she wore.

Not because of Akil's kiss, but because the dress made her feel more feminine than jeans and a shirt. She figured her hairstyle should support that feeling. When she was satisfied with her overall look she picked up her music from the table right by the door, reached for the knob and pulled it open.

"Good morning," Akil said, an unfamiliar, yet sexy, smile pulling at his lips.

Her heart leaped; the hand that was on the doorknob quickly went to her chest as if that action would stop the now-rapid beating. "Mornin'," she finally managed. "What are you doing here?"

In addition to the uncustomary smile he was wearing, his light blue jeans and royal blue sneakers that matched the royal blue T-shirt he wore were casual and unlike anything she'd seen him wear thus far. He looked different, relaxed, and she was trying to figure out why.

"Truce," he said, pulling a hand from behind his back and offering her one long-stemmed pink rose.

Her smile was instant and probably as big as the proverbial Cheshire Cat's, but she couldn't tone it down. Not while reaching for the perfectly simple, perfectly beautiful rose.

"I was just coming to meet you in the studio." As soon as the words were out she figured they weren't what he'd probably expected to hear. "I mean, thanks. I hope I'm not late for the session again."

All of a sudden she felt shy and more than a little nervous. What happened to the woman who was so sure he liked her and was just a bit proud of that fact? She'd apparently stayed somewhere in that bed, probably hiding under the sheets. Because right now she was plagued once again with the question, why?

Akil shook his head. "Nah. I figured we'd start a little later today. Give us time to get a good breakfast first. Join me?"

His extended hand stood between them and looked a little out of place since before last night he'd never touched her and she hadn't thought of touching him. Those butterflies were back, performing a whole choreographed number probably for the benefit of telling her to take his hand and go.

With a mental shrug she dropped the music she'd held in one hand onto the table by the door. Taking his hand, she put the rose to her nose and inhaled. "Breakfast sounds good."

The terrace was located on the south side of the house, so in the morning it received lots of sun. One long glass-topped table with white, high-backed chairs was shaded by the deck covering above. Still, the light morning breeze trickled inside, lifting the tips of her hair just slightly.

Akil wasn't surprised. He'd been noticing little things like that about Charlene since he'd first seen her photo. All those little things were adding up to something, he knew. Last night after she'd closed the door in his face, again, he'd felt even more disturbed. What was it about her that had him acting like a confused teenager?

Bottom line, they had two things going on here—his budding attraction to her and this CD. There needed to be boundaries so things wouldn't get out of control.

She was sitting across from him, had set the rose he gave her right beside her place setting. She kept looking at it, like it meant a lot to her. Actually, it had been an afterthought for him to bring it to her. Mrs. Williamson, for some reason, loved to have fresh flowers around the house. It didn't bother him and he was used to seeing or smelling them all around whenever he was here.

"About the last few days," he started, never being one

to beat around the bush. "Again, I want to apologize. I'm not usually that hard to work with."

"Should I consider myself special?" she asked with that smile that had warmth beginning to spread from somewhere in the southerly region of his body.

"Let's just say I needed to get a handle on a few things." She looked away from him and he wondered if once again he'd said the wrong thing. "That doesn't make you any less special. It's just that the problem was mine, not yours."

She shrugged. "So you've fixed the problem?"

Mrs. Williamson, with the young housekeeper, Nannette, following behind her with a big pitcher of orange juice, approached the table.

"Good morning. Breakfast will be served in a few minutes," she said, moving her sixty-four-year-old body as if she weren't a day over twenty-one. She was a tall woman with a thick build and a scowl that could burn a hole right through you. Delores Williamson also possessed a laugh that could touch the deepest recesses of a person's heart and the compassion to save the world if she could. She was a great woman, a great find on Akil's part. He loved her like a mother and she treated him like a son.

"Thank you," Charlene murmured as Mrs. Williamson placed a glass in front of her and Nannette quickly filled it with orange juice. She smiled at them both then lifted the glass to her mouth for a sip.

Akil nodded his head and waited until they were once again alone. "I've come to grips with a few things that were bothering me." He picked up the conversation where he'd left off.

"Oh, the fact that you didn't want to like me, for instance?"

She was smart and to the point. He liked that about her.

"I never said I didn't want to like you."

"No. You just said you didn't like me." Her head tilted a bit to the side and her eyes squinted. He couldn't tell if it was because she was studying him so hard or that the sun was getting in her eyes.

"But do you normally kiss women you don't like?" she asked.

He'd known he wasn't going to be able to avoid that question or what he'd done last night. And for the record he hadn't regretted the kiss. In fact, it had played an intricate part in the sultry dreams he'd had about her throughout the night. The ones he wasn't about to mention to her.

Clearing his throat, he replied, "I don't normally kiss women that I don't like. And I never kiss singers that I'm working with."

"Oh." She sat back in her chair as if the picture was just now clearing for her. "So, clarify something for me. Are you upset that you're attracted to someone like me or because you're attracted to a singer?"

Saying she'd hit the nail right on the head would be a cliché, but no less true. "Can I first get a clarification for the statement 'someone like me'?"

"You know, a big-boned woman. Even though I really hate that saying. Bones have nothing to do with your weight. Anyway, is that why you're upset?"

Her statement left him incredulous. He hadn't figured her for a woman with self-esteem issues surrounding her weight. Although he could see where they stemmed from. She'd grown up in L.A. where gorgeous, thin bodies seemed to fall from the sky. A woman that was outside those parameters was not the norm. Plus her own sister was a model. Yet, here on the East Coast, especially in the South, women with a little meat on their bones was the preference. Or was that a cultural thing? Did only black men appreciate a shapely woman? Maybe? Probably? But right at this moment he wasn't concerned about the generalities. He was more concerned with her and squashing any misconceptions she might be having.

"First, let me start by saying I'm a thigh man. Silicone breasts and twenty-inch waists aren't my style. So the answer is no, your physique has nothing to do with my sour attitude."

She looked as if she'd released a held breath and he was surprised to realize that's exactly what she'd assumed. He wondered if some other jackass man had made comments about her weight.

"Then it must be my singing. You don't think I can do this CD? I'm not what you want on your label? If that's the case then I don't see why you'd bring me all the way out here. I mean, if you want someone else I can easily go back to L.A., to my teaching job."

She was talking faster, pushing her chair back and standing, about to leave.

"Hold on," he said quickly, getting up himself and coming around the table to grab her arm. "Wait a second, that's not what I was thinking at all. I love your voice."

That stopped her cold and she looked up at him. "You do?"

He nodded. "Your voice is perfect. Especially for this project. I wasn't so sure at first, but that was my being shortsighted for thinking about the commercialism and the bottom lines instead of focusing on the music the way I should have."

She was shaking her head, trying to pull out of his grasp. "I don't understand."

He only moved his hands to her shoulders, holding her still and close. "When the execs at Empire called me to talk about you and what they envisioned it didn't match with what I saw in the pictures or heard on the demo. Jason was so excited after he'd heard you at the karaoke bar, he'd only told me that we'd hit it big scooping you up before any other companies could hear you. So I went into this project with one thought. Then I saw you and you were different. I didn't know how to handle it."

"And now?"

"Now I've got my focus back. I know what I want."

And Lordamercy, so did she.

She wanted Akil to kiss her again.

Instead he guided her back to her chair where she sat and tried to rein in her tumultuous hormones. She'd brought up the kiss and he'd neatly waltzed around that conversation. Instead he'd focused on explaining why he'd been so nasty to her the last few days. And while she understood what he'd said she still felt he could have handled it differently. At any rate, she was cool with letting bygones be just that.

By the time Akil had returned to his side of the table and taken his seat, Mrs. Williamson and Nannette were back with trays of food. When they were finished, after two trips to the kitchen and back, it looked like a buffet for about fifteen people.

"Does she always cook this much?" Charlene whispered to Akil when Mrs. Williamson was gone.

He grinned. "She's got it in her head that I don't eat enough while I'm away. So when I'm home she cooks enough to feed an NFL team."

Charlene nodded her agreement. "I see."

"Well, shall we?"

"Ah, just a sec," she said then bowed her head, about to bless her food.

"My mother used to do that," he said sort of absently.

Charlene paused and looked back up at him. "What? Say grace before she ate?"

"Yes."

"And you don't?"

He shrugged and looked sort of embarrassed, then said, "Not usually."

"Well, you should always give thanks for what you have. Others aren't as fortunate." When she was about to lower her head again she saw that he looked a little perplexed. So she extended her arm across the table, wiggling her fingers to signal that she wanted his hand. He gave it to her and their fingers entwined.

"Now bow your head and close your eyes."

"I know that part, Charlene."

"Oh, okay. Lord, we humbly thank You for this food that You have given. We thank and bless the hands that have prepared this meal and pray Your strength for those less fortunate. Amen."

"Amen," he said quietly, looking at her with that same puzzled expression.

"Why are you looking at me like that?"

He shook his head, then turned his attention to the fork next to the platter of bacon. "Nothing. I mean, you're just different, like I said before."

Charlene filled her plate with fluffy scrambled eggs, a few slices of melon and two spoonfuls of grits. "You make different sound bad. My mother used to do that."

His plate was overflowing by this time with eggs, French toast, bacon, sausage and a biscuit that he was now slathering with grape jelly.

"Not bad. Just different." He shrugged. "So, I take it you and your mother aren't close."

She finished chewing the bite of eggs she'd taken. "Quite the contrary, my family's pretty tight. We just don't agree all the time."

"Most people don't, family or not."

"I guess you're right. She just wanted something different for me."

"Different from teaching?"

"Yes. She wanted me to model like my older sister or get into acting since my dad was a movie and television producer."

"But you preferred singing."

"I preferred being out of the spotlight. Doing what I love in a place that's comfortable to me."

He stopped chewing and stared at her. "So this making a CD isn't what you want to do?"

"Oh, no. It is. I just never told anybody that it was a goal. I think I was afraid of the rejection or something." She stared down at her plate, kept on eating because she knew he was looking at her and it was making her nervous.

"So, you've been hiding?"

"So to speak."

"What made you come out of hiding?"

"My best friend was feeling down. I wanted to cheer her up."

"And you got a record deal out of it. How'd your best friend fare?"

The thought alone made Charlene smile. "She's

getting married next month to a man she thought wasn't her type but ended up being the love of her life."

"You think that's sweet, don't you?"

"Of course. Don't you? I mean, just because I've never personally experienced romance and falling in love doesn't mean I don't believe in it and can't rejoice when someone else finds it."

She'd said a mouthful, giving him more information than he'd asked. But he was glad. Now he knew what she needed. Only problem was, he wasn't sure he was the one who should be giving it to her.

"You've never been in love?"

"Nope." She licked her lips after taking a sip of juice and Akil felt his groin tighten.

"Never been romanced?"

"Let's see," she said, holding a forkful of melon midway to her mouth. "I've been taken to dinner, which we both paid for. Taken to a family cookout where I was asked to cook and help clean up. Oh, and this was the best one, I've been asked to wear dark glasses and a trench coat when coming to visit at his apartment."

"What? Don't tell me you did that." Anger bubbled low in his gut at the mere thought of some dude asking her to camouflage herself to come and see him.

She hurried to finish chewing. "Of course not. I knew he wasn't worth my time when I noticed he had two cell phones. The only people who should have two phones on their hips are doctors or drug dealers. And there was no M.D. after his name."

Akil's entire body tensed at her words but he hoped she didn't see. "Good. You were too good for him anyway," he said in what he hoped was a steady voice.

For a minute she looked as if she wasn't going to say anything else, as if she was almost hating what she'd admitted to him so far. That could be true since it was his perception that Charlene Quinn was very guarded about her personal life. Still, she took a deep breath and continued. It was that strength in her that he was beginning to admire immensely.

"I was too big for him is what I really think. But I'll settle for your opinion, too."

She smiled and he'd swear that action actually touched his heart. He liked talking to her, liked sitting here like this having a meal with her. He'd never shared a meal with a female in his home. Ever.

"Does it bother you? Your size, I mean."

She put her fork down and stared at him seriously. "I guess. Sometimes. Not all the time. Does it bother you?"

"No," he answered quickly.

She smiled. "Good."

"Real good," he said, lifting her hand from the table and kissing the back of it.

So, she'd never had romance, always had cornball dudes in her life. Akil decided he would fix that because she deserved it. And he wanted to be the one to give it to her.

Chapter 9

Charlene had no clue whose idea it was to have a barbecue. But on a Thursday afternoon, two weeks after the first day she'd stepped into Akil's house, once they'd finished recording for the day, they'd all headed out to the pool. She was shocked to see that the area had been transformed into what looked like an outside club.

Mrs. Williamson and the crew must have worked all day getting this set up. The thing that really shocked her was that it was a little after nine in the evening, past time for a barbecue to have started. Then again, since being in Miami and watching the way Akil worked, she was starting to think nothing was impossible.

He just had that type of presence. The one that said "I'm here now, the job can be done right." His household staff respected him and his studio staff was in awe of him. His directions were very rarely challenged—

everyone just trusted what he did or said would produce a hit.

Today's session had gone fairly well. They now had four recorded tracks for the CD—three ballads and one dance tune. As for the dance tune that had the rap portion, Akil still hadn't decided which rapper would provide the flow.

Stepping out into the humid September night, Charlene saw a few celebrity faces that included some of Akil's top contenders for the spot.

Drake, who was steadily climbing the charts with his latest hit, "Successful," featuring Trey Songz, stood near one of the two lighted bars that had been set up. He was chatting it up with none other than another superproducer, Sean "Diddy" Combs, and a scantily dressed, half-shaved-headed Cassie, who looked as if she were bored already. Young Jeezy was also there, fresh off the release of the track he'd done with Rihanna. And one of her favorites, an old-school hip-hopper who had blazed her own trails in the late eighties and early nineties, MC Lyte was there looking as classy as ever.

So while the guest list made this look like a star-studded event, the atmosphere seemed laid-back and relaxed. Just a barbecue on a fall night in Miami.

"You planning on hiding out here all night?" Jason asked, coming to stand beside her.

"No," she replied quickly. "I'm a little tired so I might just head up to bed."

But Jason was already shaking his head, grasping her hand and pulling her out of the little alcove she'd found near the entrance back into the house. "Oh, no, you don't. We're gonna kick back and relax tonight. We've been working hard, every day for two weeks now. We've earned this break."

"Yeah, but you know we still have an early session tomorrow. If I stay down here relaxing too long I'll be no good in the morning."

"Relax, Charlene. Akil wouldn't have okayed this get-together if he didn't think we all needed a break."

"Well, he's not even here," she commented, looking around and noticing that she had yet to see him out here.

"He'll be here, don't worry. Akil loves a barbecue and he loves to have company."

"He does?" She wondered at his words. "I wouldn't have guessed that."

"Akil's not the all-work-and-no-play guy you've seen so far. He can party with the best of us when he's not stressing about work. Which, unfortunately, is most of the time."

She had to chuckle at that. "Yeah, I'm definitely getting the all-work side." Except for the morning meals they'd been sharing. It was then, she thought, that she got a glimpse of the real Akil Hutton.

The Akil Hutton she was beginning to like beyond the walls of the recording studio.

He'd been watching her all night. As she smiled and shook hands, danced and laughed, he'd watched. Two hours after his little get-together had started Akil felt like a stalker standing to the side, watching Charlene as if he were obsessed.

Truth be told, he sort of was.

Not since that first day seeing her in the Empire offices had he been able to get her out of his mind. Her voice echoed in his head when he was alone, her scent hovered in his senses, keeping him awake when it was rest that he needed. This entire project had begun to revolve solely around her. He'd sent back two songs that didn't match the woman. In his eyes she was pure, radiant, terrific.

It was crazy, he knew. These feelings he had for her coming from out of nowhere. All these years he'd kept his heart under lock and key. And now, in the span of two weeks he was afraid someone—Charlene Quinn—had effortlessly picked that lock.

But it wasn't leading anywhere, his feelings for her, his desire for her. It couldn't. Hadn't he just admitted her purity? Hadn't he seen from the very start that she was different than anyone he'd ever met? No way would she be able to live with his past, with the darkness that still haunted him on a daily basis.

Still, he couldn't stand there another minute and watch another man touch her. Jason had stuck close to her most of the night, introducing her around, convincing her to dance with him. Then Five had taken a turn, bringing her a drink, talking to her while Jason escaped for a while. That was what had really pissed Akil off. While he liked Five, they'd worked together on a lot of projects and he respected the man's talent, he knew he was a dog when it came to women. That was as nicely as Akil could put it.

He'd danced with Charlene, some rap song Akil couldn't even remember now. All he remembered were Charlene's movements. The gyration of her body as she felt the rhythm. The salacious smile on Five's face as he watched and danced up close on her. Only by great strength did he manage to keep from running across the yard and driving his fist into Five's jaw. He'd actually seen red, wanted to physically remove the man from his house, from Charlene's path.

It was insane. He knew it but couldn't control it.

That's what he was telling himself as he started toward her. He couldn't control this hunger he had for her any more than he could control the weathermen predicting they'd be hit sometime tomorrow by Hurricane Viola. Couldn't control the urge to touch her, taste her, be with her. For as long as it could last.

"I need to speak to you alone," he heard himself saying as his fingers closed around her forearm.

She turned to him in shock, probably because he'd come from behind. Jason, Five, Jax and Steve—Akil's bodyguards—were sitting at the table with her talking. He'd had no clue what they were talking about, had only seen her once again surrounded by men tonight and had lost it.

He'd walked fast, wanting to get her alone as soon as humanly possible. That meant the pool house. Sure, it was kind of cheesy, sort of juvenile, especially when he had this huge house he could drag her into instead. But he didn't care and he couldn't wait. Pushing the door open, he pulled her inside. Then he slammed the door shut and backed her up against it.

She gasped, her lips falling open as she looked like she was about to say something. But his gaze had settled on her lips and heat soared through his body at a rapid pace that blurred his thinking. The next thing he knew his lips were on hers, his tongue plunging deep into her mouth.

Charlene was still reeling from the way Akil had grabbed her, all but pulling her up from her seat and dragging her across the lawn. She'd wanted to pull away, to scream at him that he was out of his mind, but something in his stance had stopped her. This wasn't the same Akil. It wasn't the man she'd watched discreetly throughout the evening, mingling with his guests, smiling here and there. It was the serious music expert she'd seen in the studio.

And more. When she'd looked up at him his eyes had been different. Those eyes that had first drawn her attention that day in the Empire offices. They seemed darker, more intense, with an edginess that almost frightened her. Her heart had immediately beat faster. She probably should have pulled away from him. Hell, maybe she should have run from him. That's how freaked out the look in his eyes made her. But she didn't.

She let him pull her along, desperately wanting to know what was on his mind. What could have put that look in his eyes? It was probably more foolish than she cared to accept, but she couldn't turn away from him. Not now.

So they were going to the pool house. Maybe he wanted to talk.

No. She swallowed that thought the moment he pushed her back to the door and his lips crashed down on hers.

Like a firestorm, heat poured into her with his touch. She struggled to breathe but realized it wasn't worth it. This kiss was all-consuming. Akil was overwhelming. Their tongues dueled as if their very lives depended on this moment. His hands were everywhere, dragging past her breasts, touching her waist, sliding over her hips, reaching around and gripping her bottom. His fingers dug into her like he was fighting to hold on, to keep her in his grasp.

His teeth raked over her swollen lips, dragged a heated path down her neck where he bit none too gently. Her head fell back, banging lightly against the door. She inhaled and exhaled frantically, her own hands roaming from his taut shoulders down his muscled back.

His touch was heated, the feel of his body beneath her fingertips electric. She whispered his name, over and over, because she was so full of him. No questions, no recriminations, just him.

He was moving downward, his tongue scraping along her chest, nipping at her nipples through her blouse. Her fingers clenched in the material of his shirt, trying to pull him back. She wanted his lips again, his tongue, everything.

But he had other ideas. Down farther, his face buried in her midsection. He mumbled something; it sounded like her name. His hands were still gripping her bottom, pulling and squeezing until heat waves floated to her center, the pulsating dampening her panties.

He moved farther down until he just passed the zipper of her slacks. He stopped there, extended his tongue and licked. His tongue moved over the linen material but she felt it as if it were her bare skin. Instinctively her legs parted.

He groaned again.

She sighed as he licked once more.

Her thighs were shaking now, her center lips throbbing incessantly. His face burrowed deeper between her legs and she thought he'd suffocate. But his breathing continued, just as ragged and frustratingly fast as her own. He continued licking as his fingers moved to the center of her bottom in a scintillating motion, up and down.

Her entire body trembled. "Akil," she cried raggedly.

She heard her voice, could barely recognize the wanton tone and was about to speak when she heard something.

It was music. No, more like a jingle. A cell phone jingle?

Akil cursed, letting his forehead rest on her thigh. Yep, it was a cell phone jingle. It was Akil's phone ringing.

With another long string of curses, he stood up, reached in his back pocket and pulled the phone out. His eyes locked with hers and she saw his lips, too, were swollen. Lifting a finger, she touched his bottom lip and felt herself moving closer, wanting—no, needing—another taste.

She kissed his bottom lip gingerly, then licked its plump surface. He groaned and leaned in closer to her, pressing his obvious arousal into her.

And that damned jingle kept playing.

"Dammit!" Akil roared. He tore his mouth away from hers and looked down at the phone.

And just like that the heat that had engulfed them just seconds ago stalled. Replacing it was a frigid breeze that came the moment he stepped away from her.

He gave her his back, pressed Talk and said, "Hello?"

When he turned back around that look in his eyes had changed and Charlene felt ten times a fool. What the hell had she been thinking, letting him paw at her, kiss on her, arouse her the way he had?

He didn't say anything. He didn't have to. Their moment was over. Whoever that was on the other end of the phone had shattered it, effectively taking all his attention.

Well, the last thing she intended to do was beg. Instead she moved away from the door, giving him the out she knew he sought.

Seconds later he'd unlocked it, walked through it and left her.

Alone.

Aroused.

And pissed the hell off!

Chapter 10

"First," she started talking the moment she stepped onto the terrace. Akil was sitting in the seat at the head of the table. He'd long since stopped sitting across from her in the morning when they shared breakfast. He sat at the head and she sat right on the end beside him.

She'd enjoyed those breakfasts. After their rocky start, these last two weeks had brought new hope for her and Akil. He was no longer acting like a year-round Scrooge and had actually smiled a time or two when Jason and his interminable silliness got out of hand. Excitement about the project was steadily brewing, within her and the rest of the Playascape staff. She was beginning to believe it was really going to happen.

The memory of last night played brightly in her mind. She'd thought about it for hours while tossing and turning. Part of her wanted to be supremely pissed off at Akil. Another part was pissed off at herself for letting things go too far.

This morning she'd awakened determined to get some things off her chest.

"Let me just clear the air," she continued. "I am not now nor will I ever be an opportunist. I'm not a groupie or some right-here-right-now chick. I don't care what impression I may have given you last night but I don't jump into bed with just anybody, even if they're about to give my music career a head start. And I don't appreciate being toyed with as if I do."

He sat back in the chair, lifting both his hands as if to say he was calling a truce. "Charlene."

She shook her head, afraid that if she didn't get it all out at once she'd chicken out. "No." Cutting him off was rude but that was nothing in comparison to what he'd done to her last night. "I'm talking. I appreciate all you're doing for me career-wise. But everything else, if you're not serious in throwing your attention my way, then I'd prefer you back off altogether. I didn't come out here for these head games you insist on playing. Truth be told, I'm tired of them."

He stood and reached for her hand but she backed up.

"Don't touch me, Akil. I'm telling you that now is definitely not the time."

Dropping his hands to his sides, he sighed in frustration. "Fine. Then would you just sit down and listen to me for a moment? I totally respect what you've said, but I have something to say, too."

She thought about it a moment. She shouldn't. Her speech had been delivered, and very well if she could say so herself. Walking away from him now would prove her point. She was just about to go when she made a fatal mistake.

She looked into his eyes.

And everything she'd been thinking, feeling, fell to the side. He didn't look angry or intense. He looked confused, broken-down almost.

Now, that could be what she'd wanted to see but she wasn't willing to let it slide.

"Well, I do have to eat breakfast," she said finally and took her seat.

He sat down, too. The morning was a little overcast with huge gray clouds moving fiercely through the sky. It unnerved Charlene a bit since the local weather forecasters had been tracking Hurricane Viola's path through the Caribbean Islands.

"Worried about the storm?" he asked and she realized she must have been looking up at the dismal sky. "It'll be fine, don't worry about it. I didn't buy a beachfront property for just that reason. We're fairly secluded out here so a heavy rain and some wind is usually all we get." Obviously she didn't look convinced because he reached out to take her hand. She pulled out of his reach. "I promise not to let anything happen to you."

"Forgive me for not putting a lot of stock in your promises," she quipped.

"I apologize for last night," he said, looking directly at her. "Not for touching you or kissing you. Not for anything that happened between you and me. Because I meant that. I wanted that." He inhaled, then exhaled slowly. "But I apologize for the phone call and for leaving the way I did. It was rude."

"It was hurtful," she amended.

He nodded in agreement. "I'm sorry. That wasn't my intention at all."

"Who was on the phone?" she asked the question she'd sworn a million times she wasn't going to ask.

And he hesitated just like she knew he would.

"It was an old friend. One that I haven't heard from in a long time and one I'm not thrilled about hearing from now."

"I see," she said, nodding.

He immediately started shaking his head. "No. You don't. It wasn't a female friend."

"Oh."

"Anyway, let's just forget about it. The phone call had nothing to do with you and I shouldn't have left the way I did. So I'm apologizing." He reached his hand out to her again. "Forgive me?"

Looking down at his upturned hand she thought of all the reasons why she shouldn't. Because he's arrogant, and more often than not rude and disconcerting, and if he really wanted her why hadn't he come back for her and…

Then the reasons why she should interrupted. He was awfully cute when he was being apologetic. Beyond the fact that he'd run out on her, he didn't really need to explain about the phone call or the friend, and she was dying to touch him, to feel the energy produced by her skin against his once more.

"I don't know why I'm doing this," she began.

She hadn't extended her hand that far before he reached out the extra length and took her hand in his. "Because you know there's something going on between us. Something you want to explore as much as I do."

"Akil, what I said before about not jumping into bed with just anybody is true."

"I know it is and despite what you might think, it's true for me, too."

She chuckled. "Then we make some pair, huh?"

"Yeah, that's what I keep thinking. Listen, I cancelled recording for today. With the weather worsening I didn't want the guys coming all the way out here and getting stuck."

He reached for his hot chocolate and took a sip. He didn't drink coffee, said it made him too jumpy and he liked to always be alert. She thought the reason was more the fact that Mrs. Williamson made it herself with whole milk and three kinds of chocolate, topped off with whipped cream and chocolate shavings, but she didn't dare say that to him.

She was a tea drinker herself, green tea or black decaffeinated with honey tasted better to her and also massaged her vocal cords. Charlene was beginning to get used to the not-so-subtle mothering of Mrs. Williamson and the other household staff.

"So what are we going to do today?" she asked, trying not to focus on the weather but instead on the platters Mrs. Williamson had already put on the table.

He shrugged. "Figured we'd just hang out, watch some movies. I don't get a lot of downtime. I should probably take advantage when I can."

"I agree. It doesn't seem like you enjoy your success much."

Still rubbing a thumb over the back of her hand, he looked at her seriously. "I'm enjoying being with you."

Seconds ticked by and she was speechless. And just when she'd thought she could talk without blabbering she heard the click of heels on the tiled floor from the direction of the kitchen.

Charlene silently cursed the end of her alone time

with Akil. And from the look on his face he was doing the same thing.

"Good morning, good people. Charlene, I've got a surprise for you," Serene's high-pitched voice was already talking the moment she stepped onto the terrace.

"Darling," she said, leaning over and kissing Akil on the cheek. He didn't look too happy to see her.

"Good morning, Serene."

"Look who I've brought with me," she said with a flourish of her long, gold bangle–covered arm. "Carlo, you remember Akil. And this is Charlene Quinn—our next project."

Charlene didn't like being referred to as a "project" but smiled through the discomfort and extended her hand to shake Carlo's.

"Mmm-hmm," he said, his fake gray eyes assessing her. "Stand up, dear." He'd taken her hand and was stepping aside so she could stand.

With a fleeting glance to Akil, who only nodded for her to comply, Charlene stood.

Carlo was almost as tall as Serene, a rail-thin man with long arms and an even longer nose. He looked either Puerto Rican or Mexican, she couldn't really tell, but his hair was slicked back with enough mousse or other hair product to shellac one of Akil's hardwood floors. He held her arm up in the air and twirled her around.

"Mmm. No. No. No." He was grumbling and mumbling some other stuff that Charlene couldn't understand before he finally let her arm down to her side.

He stood in front of her then, one arm folded over his chest, the other propped up so that his hand rested on his chin. He wore skinny jeans that accentuated the fact that he was indeed skinny and a button-down striped shirt that made her dizzy if she stared at it for too long.

"This is definitely no good," he said, lifting the edge of her ruffled blouse, which she'd worn tucked into denim capris. "Ruffles are for little girls, which you definitely are not."

Charlene tried not to bristle at his comment. He was doing his job, she told herself. But then he touched her. His long pale fingers gripped her waist, just beneath her breastbone, moving around one way and then another.

"This is the problem area. We've got to focus our work here. I think everything below this area we can work with. Pencil skirts, definitely. Leggings with long tops. Empire waists. Serene, are you writing this down?"

A glance in her direction said she hadn't been. She'd been too busy staring at Akil, who didn't look thrilled with the situation. In that moment Charlene wondered what was really between the two of them. Because while from their first meeting Serene had been what she probably considered pleasant to Charlene, in the past couple of days in the studio Serene had hovered a lot closer to Akil. Charlene hadn't yet figured out how she felt about that. No, that was wrong, she knew she didn't like it. It was crazy, she had no reason feeling territorial about Akil. They were just working together, or more like cordial friends. Even though each time she saw him she desperately wanted another one of his soul-searing kisses, she couldn't afford to fool herself into thinking they meant anything.

"I'm getting it," Serene said, hustling over to the table where she'd dropped her huge purse and pulling out a notepad and pen. "What do you think of the hair?

I'm not really feeling it. A funky cut might work," she suggested.

Carlo was already shaking his head. "No. Won't work. Too round of a face, not flattering."

Now at that, Charlene did bristle. "Now, wait just a minute," she began to protest. At her sides her fists clenched but still they continued to talk. Maybe she should just be quiet, take the bitter with the sweet. After all, wasn't this a part of the job? She'd known this would happen sooner or later. She'd just have to deal with it. Besides, Akil hadn't said a word yet. Did that mean he was backing this little assessment of Carlo's?

Embarrassment bubbled inside her. She fought against the urge to turn and run from the room or grab one of these skinny idiots by the neck and squeeze. Akil had never looked at her like some of the men she met back home. He seemed to see past the physical to something else that she was beginning to think made him happy. Last night certainly should have proved that there was something about her body he liked. Now, with Carlo's words, she wondered if that were truly the case.

"We'll keep it long, feather it. Maybe add some highlights. Definitely need to work on the makeup." He lifted one of her arms, looked down at her nails. "I think two weeks at the spa will do. Thirty to fifty pounds off is our goal. By then she'll be trimmer and we can get started on the clothes. What are we doing for choreography? PJ or Simon? Catsuits will work with thick belts at the waist just in case we can't streamline all this right away."

Charlene had heard of the spa they were referring to; it was nestled in the pretty scenic city of Monterey in California. For a small fortune, celebrities could check in, receive a handful of laxatives on a daily basis and shed the pounds they needed to act in roles they were either too old or obviously too fat to play. Or, in her instance, to create an image that wasn't her at all. That was the absolute last place she wanted to be. The thought alone made her nauseous.

Then her head was swimming, her skin heated from the combination of rage and mortification. She took one retreating step and felt light-headed.

"Hold still," she heard Carlo say.

"Copper highlights, you think?" Serene was saying.

The room was spinning, the French toast and cottage cheese she'd taken only a few bites of for breakfast flip-flopping in her stomach, threatening to backtrack. Carlo was no longer touching her but his words vibrated in her ears. Her eyes blinked but she couldn't see, everything had become blurry. She felt herself moving but couldn't tell if she were backing up on her own or if the over-the-top Carlo and Serene were pushing her.

"Enough!" Akil roared.

Silence fell quickly, as if a stripper had waltzed into a church sanctuary with her pole in hand ready to dance.

She felt a hand on her cheek. "Charlene, are you okay?"

She heard his voice and instantly began to calm down. "I...I think I need to sit down."

"Take it easy," he was saying, helping her to a chair and easing her down. Kneeling at her side, he took her hand and rubbed it gently. "Just breathe. It's okay. Just breathe."

He sounded so sure, so soothing, so she did as he said, breathing slowly in and out until her surroundings were much clearer.

"With all due respect, Akil. This has to be taken care of. The Vibe Awards are only four weeks away. We have to get started now." Serene was talking but Akil was still staring at her.

"I know when Vibe is," Akil said tightly.

"Then you know we don't have a lot of time to work with. And Carlo has other clients. We were lucky he could come by today. He's on his way to New York to work with Fantasia tomorrow."

Through clenched teeth Akil said, "He can leave now."

"What?"

Akil stood quickly, turning to face both Serene and Carlo. "Both of you can leave now. I don't need your help."

Carlo fanned a hand in front of himself as if he were about to have a heatstroke or was highly offended. Serene ran to Akil's side, lowering her voice as she said, "Akil, you know what has to be done. She's going to be a lot of work. We talked about this already."

"Yeah, Serene," Akil spoke loud enough for Charlene to hear him. "We did talk about this, on numerous occasions, and I thought I made myself perfectly clear. We're not changing Charlene's physical look. I told you maybe hair and makeup. Pick out a wardrobe that compliments, not exaggerates and not demeans. I want her image to project her as is. It's the voice we want to focus on, the music, the sound that will be different. That will sell. All this other BS is for somebody else. Not her."

Serene was shaking her head. "You've bumped your head if you think that's going to work. Maybe I need to call Sahari for further direction because you're apparently blinded by something personal."

Akil let out a small chuckle. "I'm not blinded and you can call Sahari all you want. Playascape is *my* label. Charlene is *my* artist. The final call is *mine* to make and I've just made it. Now, if you don't agree, *you* can walk. You and the beanpole over there."

At that Carlo let out something like a yelp that had Charlene jumping in her chair. She was still light-headed, but now she knew why. It wasn't Serene or Carlo's comments but her own stupidity.

Lifting a hand, she touched Akil's arm. "It's okay. I'm fine, Akil."

"Is that what you were worried about?" Serene asked in an incredulous voice. "That she was upset by what we were saying? Come on, Akil. This isn't like you. Since when does the artist have any say in how we package them? They don't know the stats we know, the pressure we're under to make back the money we invest. She's gonna have to toughen up if she's going to be in this industry."

Akil took a step closer to Serene, one that had enough tension in it that Charlene found herself struggling to stand, to hold on to his arm.

"I'm only going to tell you one more time that any decisions regarding Charlene's image will come from me. I was giving you the benefit of the doubt, thinking you had enough professionalism in you to do the job you were told to do. But I see that's not going to work. Now I want you and Carlo out of my house."

His body was trembling, with anger, she supposed. He seemed oblivious to her gentle urgings, her touch. She didn't want this to get out of hand, not because of her.

"Akil, come on, let's go into the other room. Give them a few moments."

"Oh, no, I don't need any time. You and your chubby friend can stay right here and do what you want," Carlo said in a huff. "I don't have time for the drama. I'm out."

When he was gone Serene stood looking as if steam were going to pour out of her ears at any moment. Then her glare settled on Charlene. "You won't make it past the first CD looking like that. Don't let him and his high-minded delusions of grandeur fool you. This industry will chew you up and spit you all the way back to that little vocal class in L.A. And if you're thinking that by sleeping with him you're a guaranteed success, think again. That only works for the pretty slim girls, not your kind."

Akil had reached out and grabbed Serene's arm at that point. "Goodbye, Serene."

"Don't touch me," she said tersely, pulling her arm from his grasp.

Charlene had endured lots of insults in her lifetime. She'd dealt with the mean girls in school, the boys who'd rather throw dodgeballs at her than steal kisses from her behind the bleachers in the gym. She'd listened to her mother complain about her weight, about her being the only one in the family not on the fast track to a great career. She'd watched her father's sadness when her mother spoke about her that way and also listened to Candis and Rachel as they'd told her she was a good person.

None of that seemed to matter now. All of it swirled into a funnel, slipping away in the wind, compared to the mean insults out of Serene's mouth. The main one being that Charlene wasn't even good enough to sleep her way to the top.

There was no hole in the floor that would graciously

open and swallow her up. No glittering red shoes that she could click and instantaneously be transported back home. No, there was nothing she could do to hide her humiliation at what had just transpired. And even worse, nothing she could do to stop her knees from buckling and Akil's sympathetic arms from catching her before she could make contact with the floor.

Chapter 11

"She's gonna be just fine, Akil. Stop pacing or you'll run a path in the carpet," Mrs. Williamson quipped.

But he couldn't stop. He heard her words, trusted what she was saying, but still his heart pounded as he worried about the unknown. One minute they'd been having a nice peaceful breakfast, the ones he'd come to enjoy so much in the past few days. And the next Serene and her sidekick had barged in running their mouths until he'd felt bad for Charlene and wanted to murder them both.

Then she looked ill, not agitated or hurt or angry, but sick. Her skin had paled and she'd become unsteady, wobbling until he was sure she was going to fall on the floor. Rushing to her side had been late on his part. He should have stopped Carlo and Serene the moment they came in. He knew how they both could be, especially together, using their combined half-witted brainpower.

His fists clenched, he wanted to hit somebody or something. He could have beat the feminine nature out of Carlo for the nasty things he'd said to Charlene because, after all, he was a male on the surface. As for Serene, this wasn't the first time he'd wanted to ignore the teachings about not hitting a woman just to shut her the hell up. But to hell with both of them. His only concern now was Charlene and the way she still looked too pale, and too vulnerable, sitting on the couch in the living room.

That's where he'd carried her when she'd been unable to stand on her own a moment longer. He'd called for Mrs. Williamson, who'd quickly called for Nannette, sending the younger girl up to Charlene's room. She'd brought back a pill bottle and Mrs. Williamson had continued to wipe Charlene's forehead with a wet cloth. "Get the other bottle out of the first aid kit in the kitchen, the smelling salts."

He'd frowned at that, thinking smelling salts were only used in the movies and weren't real. But he'd known better than to correct Mrs. Williamson.

"But she's not unconscious," Akil said, slightly confused.

"It's all right, the salts will bring her around. She's still a bit dazed. And she's tired. Aren't you, baby?" she asked Charlene, rubbing a thick cocoa-brown hand over Charlene's smaller, lighter one.

"Here you go," Nannette said upon her return, offering Mrs. Williamson a brown bottle with no label on it.

"How do you know that's the right one?"

"Because I make it myself," she answered tightly,

unscrewing the top from the bottle and pouring the liquid onto a dry cloth.

Akil wasn't sure he'd heard correctly. "You make drugs in my house?"

She cut an angry look at him. "I'm from the South, Akil. I've been making my own remedies since I was a young'un working at my grandma's side. It's nothing but ammonium carbonate and perfume. When the ammonium is mixed with either water or salt it creates fumes," she said, passing the cloth right beneath Charlene's nose.

"The fumes irritate the lining of the nose, throat and lungs. That's what makes them wake up from a dead faint."

On the chair Charlene yanked her head back, frowning from the smell.

"There you go. That's a good girl," she said, passing Nannette the cloth and rubbing Charlene's cheek.

"I'm fine. Really, none of this is necessary, I just need to—" Charlene was trying to talk but Mrs. Williamson wasn't trying to hear it.

"I've got your medication," Mrs. Williamson said, opening the pill bottle Nannette had brought down from Charlene's room. "You forgot to take it this morning, didn't you?"

Looking away from Akil, Charlene answered quietly, "Yeah."

Mrs. Williamson nodded knowingly. "I thought so. You know you have to eat and you have to take this every day. Hypothyroidism is nothing to play with."

"Hypo-what?" Akil asked, not knowing what either of them was talking about. "You're on medication?"

He didn't know how he felt about that but Charlene's frantic look said she had no intention of ever telling him about the meds or whatever her condition was. That pissed him off to no end.

"Why didn't you tell me?"

"Hush, Akil. That's too many questions for this girl right now. Here, sit up," Mrs. Williamson instructed Charlene. "Nannette, give me that water. Now, I want you to take this and lie here for a bit and get some rest. You've been working nonstop since you got here. A shame you're pushin' this girl like this. She needs to rest, Akil, not be yelled at or questioned to death."

With Mrs. Williamson's words, Akil dropped Charlene's hand and backed away.

She didn't need him. Mrs. Williamson was taking care of her and obviously knew more about Charlene than he did. Even though he'd thought they were growing closer with each day they spent together, he'd been wrong. She hadn't trusted him with this one detail.

He continued to back out of the room. The similarities were too eerie, too strong for him to dismiss. Panic ripped at his chest as he remembered the outcome of Lauren and her lies and omissions. The same could happen to Charlene. In this industry anything was possible. History could repeat itself.

He was sweating, his brow was damp and so were his palms, as he walked into the foyer, stopping at the steps and trying to figure out where he wanted to go.

Fears from the past engulfed him, wrapping securely around a face from the present, around Charlene. He couldn't handle it. Couldn't breathe here. Couldn't stand the possibilities.

Not again. Not ever again is what he'd promised himself. Looks like he'd failed once more.

Enough is enough, Charlene thought hours later. She'd been closed up in her bedroom by Mrs. Williamson, who had brought her lunch and a snack and warned her that dinner was coming soon. Charlene wanted to tell her it wasn't food she needed, but hadn't had the heart. She got the impression the older woman didn't get enough chance to fuss over people with Akil not living here most of the year. So she'd sat back and let her go at it. Truth be told, she had been just a little tired. The long hours in the studio were beginning to take their toll. She was actually glad when Akil said he'd cancelled today's session.

But that was before the scene on the terrace. Before she was embarrassed out of her mind, then swept off her feet by her own idiocy. She'd been in such a hurry to get down to breakfast this morning she hadn't taken her medication. All the time she'd sat with Akil eating and talking she hadn't felt any different. Apparently the stress of Serene and Carlo's appearance coupled with her normal bouts of fatigue was just too much to bear. Mrs. Williamson had an auntie in North Carolina who suffered with thyroid problems, she'd told Charlene. That's how she knew what the medication was the first time she'd seen it in Charlene's room, and that's how she knew just what to do to take care of Charlene.

Admittedly it had felt good to just rest and wait for her meals. Charlene wasn't a lazy person and the staff at home was usually so busy running around at her mother's every command that they'd barely paid any attention to her.

So the day had passed quietly, night sneaking over them with just a light drizzle beginning to fall. The wind blew hard; she could tell because if she got close to the window she'd hear the whistling sound. The water in the pool rippled but Nannette, Cliff, the driver, and Yucatan, the yardman, had gathered all the lounge chairs and tables and brought them into the house. She suspected the terrace had been cleared, too, although she hadn't been back downstairs since earlier today.

But none of that kept her mind off Akil. They really were a pair. Since the day they'd met, one of them was always storming off, angry at the other. It was beginning to be their routine.

He'd seemed so upset with her when he'd left this morning. Upset that she hadn't told him about her medication. Truth be told, she hadn't seen a reason to. Her illness was *her* business. Akil was just her producer. If she was singing and giving the performance he wanted, why did he need to know? Right?

Then why did she still feel the need to explain? Climbing out of bed, she grabbed the beige silk robe that matched her nightgown and tied it around herself. Pushing her feet into her slippers, she headed straight to the door. There was no way she'd be able to sleep with this unresolved situation between them.

It was a little after ten and she'd assumed he would be in the studio, but as she stepped into the hallway she could hear music coming from the other end of the hall. The end where Akil's suite was located. Taking a deep breath, she moved in that direction, pausing at the door to knock.

After two additional knocks and no answer she figured he couldn't hear over the music so she tried the doorknob. It was open so she walked inside.

His space was twice the size of her room. Upon entering she figured she was in what should have been the sitting room. Instead of a chaise longue, coffee table and maybe a bookcase, Akil had gym equipment in this space. A weight bench, free weights, elliptical, treadmill, you name it, he had it. Walking through the room, she touched a hand to the elliptical, picturing him using the machine. She lifted a free weight and almost sank to the floor herself, it was so heavy. No wonder his arms were so muscled, if he was lifting these every day.

The music playing was that instrumental piece he'd been listening to that night in the studio, the one she had said was the journey between man and woman, the journey to falling in love. She hadn't shared the latter with him, but after hearing the song in her mind the rest of the night instead of being able to sleep, that's what she'd finally settled on.

Two steps separated the sitting room from Akil's bedroom and as she took them she immediately felt nervous. She was in his bedroom, in his personal space without permission. She didn't know how he would feel about that but assumed he would be no more upset with her than he already appeared. The room was dim but her gaze couldn't miss the king-size four-poster bed sitting on a platform to the far left. It was huge, clearly large enough for more than one person. And it was formidable, so much so that she couldn't really picture Akil sleeping there. A week ago she'd have never doubted this was where he slept, but after getting to know him better all this, the house, the private jet, the cars, seemed beyond Akil the man. There was only the music, that was the one thing that she knew suited him perfectly.

"I see you're feeling better," he said and she jumped at the sound of his voice behind her.

Spinning around, she saw that he was sitting in one of two black leather recliners that faced the wall, which was actually an entertainment center. There was a table between the recliners where the only lamp was perched.

"Ah, yeah, I'm feeling much better," she said, taking a tentative step toward him.

"Good. We'll get back to work maybe Sunday. I want to give this storm a chance to blow over."

So they were back to the cool formal tones again. Her need to talk to him faltered a bit. This was ground she'd assumed they already covered. Well, she'd just say what she had to say and leave. She wasn't in the mood for Akil's roller-coaster moods.

"I have hypothyroidism. It's when there's insufficient production of thyroid hormone by the thyroid gland. A couple of the symptoms are fatigue and weight gain. I have to take a medication called Levoxyl every day to help keep the levels up. If I skip a dose I'm really light-headed and even more tired than usual. That's what happened today. I forgot to take my medication."

He remained quiet and she kept her hands folded together in front of her. Suddenly she felt very vulnerable and almost foolish. What was she thinking coming into his bedroom, dressed in her nightclothes and giving him a lesson in the thyroid glands? Foolish, that's what she was.

"So anyway, I just figured I owed you an explanation. I guess I'll stay out of your way until Sunday."

She had already turned to go when his voice stopped her.

"Why didn't you tell me before?"

She didn't turn back to him but answered anyway. "I didn't think it was important."

"It is. Important, I mean," he said.

Her palms had begun sweating, which was unusual for her. Usually her skin was really dry. That was another effect of her illness.

"I didn't know. I guess I didn't think about it. I'm

just so used to dealing with it that I don't talk about it much."

"How long have you had this condition?"

Refusing to continue this conversation with her back facing him, Charlene turned. He was still sitting in the chair, still staring at the wall.

"We found out when I was sixteen. When my mother was tired of me failing on every diet she could come up with."

"She wanted you to lose weight, too?" he asked, a hint of incredulity in his voice.

"I've always been overweight, even as a baby. She thought it would change with time, but when it didn't she tried other ways. Until the doctor told her there was no use. The most common symptom to hypothyroidism is weight gain and water retention. So even if I starved, which was never in my nature, I would most likely be overweight."

"I thought a couple times at breakfast that you didn't eat a lot. I wondered if you were dieting but didn't want to bring it up."

"Oh, no. I'm not dieting. I just try to watch what I'm eating before I sing. Some foods just aren't good for the voice at any time. And others just make singing for long periods of time uncomfortable and most often cause missed notes. Believe me, I eat." She smiled.

He chuckled. "I'm glad to hear that."

He looked up at her then. "I wouldn't want you to starve or diet. Like I told Serene, I like you just the way you are."

Her throat was dry. Did it seem hot in here? "You didn't tell Serene that. You told her your plan for my image had changed."

Nodding his head, he finally stood and walked toward

her. "My plan for your image did change. But I've always liked the way you looked. From the picture you sent with the demo CD and the first day I met you in L.A. with your agent hovering about and Jason and Sahari seeing dollar signs. I liked the way you looked."

"Really?" It wasn't possible. Well, it could be. She didn't believe it. The great Akil Hutton liked the way she looked.

He smiled. "You sound surprised."

"I am. I mean, most men, even ones not in the business, have a certain vision of the women they like."

"That's true. And you happen to fit my vision."

Yeah, it was hot. Charlene was warm all over and when he took her hands in his she thought she'd just melt at his feet. He led her to the recliner where he'd been sitting and eased her down. "Mrs. Williamson would kill me if she knew I had you standing up all this time."

"I understand I'm no Beyoncé or Ciara. And it's fine if you can't market me and this CD doesn't become a hit. I'm just glad for the opportunity to work with you and to actually live a part of a dream I've held close for so long."

He was shaking his head, holding both her hands in his. "Have you seen Beyoncé lately? She's not all skin and bones. The public really appreciates a bootylicious figure and they're going to love you." He chuckled. "I don't want you to be like anybody but Charlene Quinn. That's the singer I'm working with and that's the woman I'm going to market. End of story."

Charlene sighed with relief and sat back in the chair. "Serene's not going to be happy to hear that."

"Serene's fired so it doesn't really matter what she likes."

"Oh, no. You're firing her? Because of me? I don't want to cause that type of trouble."

"You didn't cause it. You just brought it to a head. Things have been brewing with us for a while. She's blinded by the dollar signs and notoriety."

"And what are you doing? You know what the trend is now, you know what the listeners want. Why are you so sure it'll work if you take a chance and do something different with me?"

"Because when you sing I can feel it here." He'd taken her hand and guided it to his chest, rested it over his heart. "No singer has affected me that way in years. What you have is true and it's pure. It's the soul of music and that's what I want to record."

Charlene didn't know what to say or how to react. She tried to take a deep breath, licked her lips and gave a nervous smile. "I'm flattered," she said honestly.

His smile was different than any she'd ever seen on him before. It touched his eyes until he looked like he could really be happy for once. "I'm honored to be working with you on this project."

With that he lifted her hand from his chest, brought it to his lips and kissed the tip of each one of her fingers.

"I'm thankful to have finally met someone as honest and real as you. In this business that's hard to find."

She could relate to what he was saying. She was thankful for Rachel for that very reason. True friends, sincere connections, were hard to come by when you had money, fame, prestige, or all three.

"More importantly," he was saying, his kisses having moved to the center of her hand, where his tongue swirled over her skin until tingles of pleasure soared through her body, resting quite suddenly in her center,

"I just cannot seem to get you out of my mind. And since the first time I kissed you, you've become like a drug. My own personal addiction. Damn, I'm dying to kiss you," he finished with his tongue scraping over her wrist, kissing up her arm as the wide-armed material of the sleeve on her robe slid downward.

"Oh," was all she could manage. Had he been reading her mind? Sure, she'd come here to talk to him, to explain what had happened, but she'd wanted him. For days now she'd known she wanted Akil, and last night had only brought that need to a head.

The aggressor in sexual encounters she was not. And so she'd resigned herself to wait until he'd made a move like he was interested in her in *that* way. Well, coupled with last night in the pool house and now watching the swirl of his tongue on the heated skin of her inner arm, she could safely say that he was.

"I apologize for being so harsh and behaving like a greedy teenager last night. I can be better," he said, giving her just the barest hint of a smile. "Can I kiss you, Charlene?"

Hell, yeah! her mind screamed even as the slow melodic tune still blared from his speakers. Luckily she had a little bit of control left. She would not act like a desperate, horny female aching for his touch.

However, considering she hadn't had sex in over a year and her hormones had been racing at the simplest thought of Akil since the time he'd kissed her, that's exactly what she was.

"Yes, you ca—"

Her words were cut off, her breath stolen and the world as she'd known it officially shaken as Akil's lips

descended upon hers in an action that was not soft and
not slow, but was full of as much passion and energy as
the first roars of thunder crackling outside his bedroom
window.

Chapter 12

From the steady thumping water against the window she'd say the light drizzle had picked up. Winds were still blowing as Miami sat waiting to go through round one with Hurricane Viola.

While inside Akil's bedroom Charlene waited for something else.

His kisses had the effect of a drug, making her limbs weak, her body compliant and her sex hot with anticipation. Her hands had gripped his taut shoulders as he'd slanted his head, deepening the kiss until it felt as if their mouths had been fused together. His tongue persistently stroked hers, his hands cupping her face with a gentle touch that didn't match the intensity of the kiss.

Her mind whirled as sensations poured into her. On the one hand she wanted nothing more than to continue kissing Akil. The feel of his lips, the taste of his tongue, the touch of his hands so soft on her face, all of this was pleasurable. Enough so that her knees quaked, closing as her thighs squeezed tight to tamp down on the growing pressure in her center.

On the other hand, she wanted more than she'd ever wanted before. This need that burned inside of her was new and intense, causing her entire body to tremble, her breath to come in erratic spurts.

"Akil," she managed a whisper when he'd pulled back slightly to suckle her bottom lip.

On a ragged moan, he murmured, "I can't stop wanting you."

"You don't have to stop," she heard a voice say but wasn't sure it was her own.

His hands moved down her neck to cup each of her breasts. It was her turn to moan and to squirm once more against the force of need boiling inside. Her body was hot, like liquid fire ran through her veins. When he flicked his fingers over the tight nipples of her breasts she almost screamed. Between her legs her clit throbbed and her head fell back on the chair as she tried to swallow, tried to get a grip on these raging emotions.

"No," he said adamantly. "I want you to look at me when I touch you."

At his words her head snapped up, her eyes wide open. He was beautiful with his eyes half-closed, his long fingers gripping and squeezing her full breasts. Leaning forward, he breathed over one taut nipple that she felt puckering even more through the thin material of her robe and gown. As if the material weren't there at all his tongue extended, rubbed over the nipple once, twice, until the material was damp and so were her panties.

His name tore from her lips as she gripped his shoulders, her chest heaving, legs holding tighter together.

"Tell me what you want," he said, moving to the other nipple, taking it between his teeth and biting lightly.

"Oh. My." She couldn't even finish the thought, let alone do what he'd asked of her.

"Do you want me to take your clothes off?" he asked, flattening his body against her the best he could, considering she was sitting in the recliner.

His broad chest brought a new heat against her midsection. His strength pressing into her thighs ignited the fire already brewing in that region and she felt herself pressing into him desperately.

"Do you want to be naked?" His voice was more urgent, strained with what she could only assume was desire. "You naked? Me naked? Me touching you, tasting you? Tell me, Charlene. What do you want?"

"Yes," she almost screamed but ended with a guttural moan that sounded more animalistic than human.

Akil didn't waste a second after her answer. His hands worked quickly, untying the robe, pulling it from her shoulders. Then he lifted the hem of her gown and waited as she lifted slightly from the chair so he could pull it over her head. She never slept in a bra, so her panties were next to go. Feeling a wave of self-consciousness hit, she regretted her emotion-filled answer to becoming naked. The table with the lamp on it wasn't quite four feet away. The balmy gold light poured into the room, placing her and her body on unfettered display for Akil.

As her heart continued to pound and she wondered how she could maneuver herself to the bed, to the sheet she could use to camouflage some of her not-so-alluring body parts, she caught Akil's gaze.

He was standing, looking down at her as she lay sprawled naked on the recliner. Only he wasn't looking at her body, his eyes were fastened on hers. "You're beautiful, Charlene. Don't ever let anybody tell you or make you feel differently."

Even through the heavy haze of sexual tension she felt the softness of his words, the tenderness of sincerity prick her heart. She didn't answer because his eyes had moved from hers to venture down her torso. In the dimness she could still see the shift. His normally dark, intense eye color had darkened even more, shading with a haze of lust and something else she couldn't decipher.

Not knowing what else to do and unnerved by his concentrated examination, she lifted her arms to him. If he was kissing her she wouldn't be nervous. When he touched her she felt safe, wanted. And if she could only have this moment, this night as a storm raged outside, if this was the only time she'd have Akil to herself, then she wouldn't waste a moment.

"Take off your clothes and come to me," she said and knew it was the arousal talking. Never in her life had she been this open and willing with a man. Then again, she'd never been with a man like Akil before. A man whose sheer presence spoke of power and strength and at the same time compassion. Yes, there was a part of Akil that she'd seen on occasions when they were together that said he had a softer side, a side he didn't show often. What would it be like if she were the one he chose to open up to?

He was already doing as she'd asked. Removing his clothes in a slow and precise manner, all the while keeping his eyes on her. It was kind of erotic, especially since at that moment she remembered the music playing in the background. It had changed from the first instrumental piece to another one that didn't sound familiar but cast an oddly sensual vibe around the room. So they had music, they had a stormy night and two almost naked adults. This was a perfect combination.

His thumbs were on the rim of his sweatpants, his chest already bare, when he paused and asked, "What are you thinking?"

Hmm, was this a trick question? She was definitely thinking he had one banging set of abs. Ripped didn't quite describe him as her gaze roamed over his succulent chest. She'd known his arms were tight, probably could be considered cannons for a man of exactly six feet and medium build. His pectorals were tight, the nipples erect. Her mouth watered.

"Um, I'm thinking what's taking you so long?" That was an honest enough answer, she figured.

He smiled. "Okay. Just making sure we're on the same page here."

"What page is that?"

"The one where we spend the entire night making each other feel real damn good." As he spoke he'd pushed the pants down, simultaneously stepping out of the tennis shoes he wore.

She swallowed hard, almost lost the little bit of courage she'd garnered from his earlier words. If she thought the top half of him looked good, then the bottom was definitely a prizewinner. Long muscled legs sprinkled with black hair. He turned to the side, kicking his clothes out of the way. His butt was absolutely to die for, tight and just handful-size. She thought of Will Smith in the early scenes of *I, Robot*. Akil had him beat by about a million more sweat glands reacting in her body. He turned back to face her and she heard herself gasp and wanted to crawl beneath the chair instead of sitting in it.

The phrase "he was hung like a horse" was crass, so she chased it out of her mind. Still, he was no lightweight in the size department and her body wanted more.

"I'm glad we both like what we see," he said in that cocky, arrogant tone he used more often than not. Usually it rubbed her the wrong way. Tonight it massaged every horny inch of her.

She could only lick her lips in response. Nervousness was coming back, claiming a spot right in the center of her chest. Was she in over her head with Akil? Surely he was more experienced in the sex department than she was. While both of them admitted to not just sleeping with anyone she was almost positive Akil Hutton had had more than three lovers in his whole life. His every movement spoke of sex, like he was advertising the ride of a lifetime a woman could expect from him. She wondered if she were really ready for all this.

"You wanna know what I really like about you, Charlene?" he asked, coming closer to her, going down on his knees in front of her once more.

"What?" Her voice seemed smaller or was the music in the background, the wind outside, louder?

"These," he said, his palms resting softly on her thighs.

That wasn't possible. The most hated part of her body was his favorite? She couldn't even speak.

"I knew the moment I saw you they'd be soft. I like a woman with real legs, not twigs."

At his words said legs quivered and his smile grew even wider. "Oh, yeah, that's what I'm talking about."

With his palms sliding down to her inner thighs, he pushed her legs apart, as far as they would go within the confines of the chair. Even that was far enough as she felt air over the damp skin of her center. On display for him suddenly had a new meaning.

"And I'll bet you're even softer there." His hands moved up higher, his fingers touching her swollen lips softly. "I've dreamt of touching you here, tasting you here." He looked up at her and while her eyes were dangerously close to shutting his heated glare kept them open.

"Do you taste good, Charlene?"

She couldn't even think of an answer to that question. Instead her fingers clenched the arm of the chair, her teeth sinking into her lower lip as anticipation tore through her.

Up and down his fingers stroked until she shivered. His hands were between her legs, touching her more intimately and openly than she'd ever been touched before. A fingertip grazed the tightened bud of her center and she sucked air in through her teeth. For seconds he played there, stroking her now-drenched lips, tweaking her tight and puckered clit. She squirmed and lifted her hips in request for more.

"Yeah," he moaned, his gaze fixed between her legs. "You're gonna taste damn good, baby girl."

Charlene couldn't think, her mind was so completely wrapped around the pleasure he was evoking. She'd thought momentarily about how wickedly wanton she must look, naked in a chair, legs gaping open, greedy hips moving incessantly. But she couldn't stop, didn't want to stop.

When she thought she couldn't take any more, his fingers slipped into her entrance, stroked, found a particularly sensitive spot and worked there until she was panting and writhing beneath him.

"Not yet," he whispered, his warm breath fanning over her thighs as he kissed his way up to her center. "Not yet."

When he arrived, his tongue took over the steady stroking of his fingers, licking up and down her lips with an efficiency that should be patented. It wasn't long before his tongue found the nub he'd touched with such perfection. Heat swirled through Charlene until she felt like she was outside in the twisting, surging wind of the brewing hurricane. If this continued she was going to explode, she knew it with certainty.

And with all her sighing and moaning, Akil probably knew it, too.

While his fingers worked her, pumped deep inside of her, his touch tortured the outer realm. She was delirious with pleasure.

"Come for me, baby girl. Now," his voice rasped over her sensitive skin, sending off a rocket-like explosion deep inside her body.

She trembled from her head to her toes, her fingernails dug into the arms of the chair and his name tore from her throat in lyrical notes not registered on any scale.

She was wrapped tightly around him as Akil moved from the chair to the bed. Her arms held him unyieldingly, like he was the only one in her world. He relished that feeling, held it as close to his heart as he could.

She sang his name and it had been the sweetest song he'd ever heard. Even the sweet taste of her orgasm, the swelling of his ego the moment she took that final plunge, none of that compared to the sweet sound of her voice, the high pitch of his name echoing throughout his bedroom. He'd kissed her then, after the last tremors of pleasure had torn through her body, after he'd felt steady enough himself to move. His lips had captured hers in a slow dance of sorts, a promise of more, an agreement of forever.

Laying her on his bed as gently as possible, Akil took a few moments just to stare down at her. This woman that he'd known for less than a month, who'd come into his life with a powerhouse voice, a mouthwatering body and the persona of a simple, naive schoolteacher. This woman that in such a short period had turned out to be so much more.

As he stood at the side of the bed she rolled over toward him, reached for his heavy erection and stroked him. His breath caught and not even the ever-growing storm outside could make him tell her to stop.

The softness of her hands produced a steady heat against his shaft and soon he was moving to her rhythm. When she looked up at him, her eyes seeking permission, he knew he had to do something. Leaning over, he reached into his nightstand, pulled out a condom and passed it to her. Intelligence was something he'd immediately known she possessed. Her fingers moved swiftly, opening the packet, removing the condom then smoothing the latex down his rigid length.

"Lie back," he whispered when he knew she would continue stroking him.

She did as he asked and he climbed on the bed, using his knees to spread her legs wide. Touching two fingers to her already wet center he stifled a moan and looked into her face as he spread her juices over the latex. Her gaze followed his fingers. He swore he grew harder just knowing she watched so intently.

Slipping his arms under her knees, he lifted her legs until her feet were planted firmly on the bed. Reaching up, he grabbed one of the pillows from beside her head and tucked it securely under the base of her back.

He positioned the thick head of his arousal at her center, but looked up at her before pressing forward.

"Thank you," he whispered.

She looked momentarily perplexed. "For what?"

"For choosing me."

As the soft smile touched her lips Akil pressed slowly inside her. Tight muscles gripped him just like her arms had wrapped around his neck. She pulled him in, deeper and deeper, until he felt like they'd been fused together.

Being inside her felt so good he had to grit his teeth. Then he kissed her lips, sucked her tongue into his mouth and moaned. "You taste good. You feel good. So damn good, baby girl."

His kisses trailed down her neck, to her breasts where he found a pert nipple and suckled like a baby. All the while his strokes grew deeper, her hips moved with his rhythm, music played in the background and for the first time in a long time, Akil also wanted to sing.

The emotion was dangerous; it was spreading in his chest like a cancer. He'd recognized it the moment he'd been alone with her. Had fought it like a boxer fighting for a title. But it wasn't working. He was falling for her and falling fast.

She wouldn't stay, he thought, even as his name again fell from her lips. She was grasping the sheets of the bed, thrashing against his brutally slow stroking. He liked it slow and deep, liked the feel of her muscles gripping him. He wouldn't go faster, wouldn't rush this moment.

Her hips moved, circled, jutted up to meet his stroke. To hurry him along. "Slow, baby girl. I like it nice and slow."

"I can't," she whimpered, her head thrashing about the pillows.

"Shhhh," he said, rising to her face, touching her lips with a light kiss. "You feel so good I don't want to stop. I don't want this to be over. Baby—"

His words drifted, his stroke deepened. He palmed her bottom, clutched the plush cheeks in his palm and thrust into her again and again. Her breasts moved with their motions, making his shaft harder, his arousal more intense. Her creamy thighs pillowed against his own and his spine tingled.

She watched him, watched them, her gaze sliding down to where they were joined. He pulled out slowly, let her look her fill. Then slid in with a little more speed, a lot more intensity and watched her eyes darken. Using his fingers he touched her plump lips, pulled them apart and slid inside of her once more. He liked to look himself, liked to see where their bodies met, joined, where he lost himself inside of her.

They both watched as the crescendo climbed. The storm outside raged a little harder, the wind rattling louder against the windows, the rain coming down in heavier sheets. The music had even changed, the song still instrumental but the tempo a little more fevered. His hips matched the moment, moving faster, riding on the impending waves of pleasure.

When he came, she came. When she came, she sang. When they both came, the music mixed with the storm. It was a symphony of pleasure, a composition of delight.

It was all he'd ever wanted.

All he ever needed.
And it was probably going to end.
Soon.

Chapter 13

Charlene had never been on the receiving end of oral sex. Until Akil.

She'd never showered with a man. Until Akil.

And she'd never in her wildest dreams thought she'd desire a man the way she did him. They'd rested for a few minutes after the intense round of sex. She'd almost called it something else but was too afraid to hope. Then he'd rolled over, chuckling and grabbing her up in his arms. They'd ended here in this shower stall built for about six people. There were benches along two of the walls and two shower heads. The blue marble reminded her of the ocean, the flecks of silver of the stars in the evening sky. It would have been relaxing if Akil weren't in there with her, intent on bathing her.

"I've been bathing myself for quite some time," she'd said, trying to move out of his grasp.

"Yeah, but this is much more fun."

"No, really, I'd rather do it myself."

He grabbed one of the arms she'd put up to ward him off, his look a little more serious. "Why? What are you afraid of?"

"I'm not afraid of anything."

"Okay, so you're uncomfortable? Nervous? Why, after what we've just shared?"

A logical question, she thought. Unfortunately she didn't have a logical answer. Her feelings just were. "I normally shower alone."

He nodded. His skin looked like a root-beer soda, glossy, wet, tempting. His sex, even at half-mast, still very impressive. "So, I'm making you nervous by being in here with you, looking at you, wanting to touch you."

She crossed her arms over her breasts, shifted from one foot to the other. "I'm just not used to it."

"Okay. That's fair." He took a slow step toward her. "But listen to this, I like the way you look. I like the way you feel in my arms. You're a strong, confident woman who can do anything she puts her mind to. I think you can shower with me and I think you can like it."

She thought he was a damn good talker. Her heart warmed at his words and her body trembled at his glare. But old habits died hard.

"Take a deep breath and prepare yourself to be touched and looked at on a regular basis because I like it."

"You can be quite cocky, Akil Hutton," she said, silently admitting to herself that she did kind of enjoy him looking and touching.

He was up close now, pulling her arms from her chest, placing them at her sides. "I know, been like that since I was a kid."

"Then I'll bet you didn't have a lot of friends."

He was rubbing his fingers along the sides of her breasts. "Friends are overrated."

"Just regular friends or girlfriends?"

He smiled, dipped his head down to run his tongue over her nipple. "You trying to ask if I've got a girlfriend, Charlene?"

"I'd like to think after what we just did and what you're currently doing that the answer is no."

He bit her nipple, then turned to adjust the spray of water. "I knew you were smart. Now can you wash my back."

She couldn't help but smile. This was the side of Akil she'd thought was there, lying just beneath the ruffled surface he displayed for everyone else. It was the part she wanted all to herself, she thought with a slap of honesty.

Reaching for the soap, she lathered it in her hands and proceeded to bathe him. Another first for her, but she was beginning to think that doing new things with this man wasn't so bad at all.

"I didn't have a lot of friends growing up because enemies came easier," Akil spoke into the darkness of his bedroom.

They'd finished their shower hours ago, the music had been turned off but the rain still beat against the windows. She was cuddled against him in his big bed, where they'd been lying just talking.

"I used to think the same thing," she admitted.

"We lived in a corner house on one of the worst streets in the city. The sound of gunshots lulled me to sleep and the smell of crack being smoked through a pipe woke me up."

She was quiet. Her childhood had been vastly different.

"I went to school every day, or at least tried to. Not too many kids on our block did. Their parents were too busy gettin' high, sticking somebody up or pimpin' their bodies for a hit to even care. But I knew it was my ticket out."

"When did you get into music?"

He sighed. "I was always into music, or should I say music was always in me? My dad was a trumpet player before he got shot up for not paying his dealer. My moms, she was a singer. Great voice, sometimes I still hear it. So I guess it's in my blood."

"That's sad. I'm so sorry, Akil."

"Don't be. You didn't put the drugs in his hand, make him get high or make him let my mother do the same." She felt his shoulders shrug. "Anyway, I always knew what I wanted to do. I wanted to make music. So I went to school, I did what they told me to graduate. Then I stalked one of the reps at Empire until they gave me an internship. And now I'm here."

"And now you're only one of the five hottest producers on the scene. Very impressive."

"Yeah, but I wish Lauren was with me."

At the mention of a female's name Charlene stiffened.

"No, it's not like that. But I like that you'd get jealous so quick." He kissed her forehead and she settled down.

"Lauren's my younger sister. Younger by seven years. We have different fathers. Mine was dead and buried by the time my mother found Lauren's. And Lauren was cutting her first tooth by the time hers disappeared."

Wow, Charlene thought to herself, such sadness

and despair all his life. No wonder he was cranky all the time.

"Lauren could sing. I mean really sing. You remind me a lot of her, your range and clarity. She was going to be big."

"What happened to her?"

"Life happened, I guess. Lauren wanted to sing, she wanted to make it big, to have money and nice things. Since we didn't have that growing up, it was like a lifeline to her. She was impatient, always had been. Impulsive and reckless. I tried to keep her on the right track, or at least that's what I thought I was doing. When I went to work at Empire I kept her up-to-date on the trends on what they were looking for, but I wanted her to at least finish high school first. There's nothing out here worth ditching your education for. Lauren disagreed.

"She latched on to some neighborhood rapper who'd just inked a deal with Sony. His records climbed the charts and he kept Lauren on his arm. Overnight she went from a high school student with a smart-ass mouth to a certified rapper's girl with shiny cars, lots of bling and scanty clothes. Darian 'MacD' Jackson was going to put her on to a record deal, just as soon as he got established. But the more money he made the less time he had to work on her career. He wanted her right where she was, under his thumb. I tried to talk to her and she kicked me out of her apartment, said I was jealous, trying to bring her down. I shrugged it off, left her to make and clean up her own mess."

This sigh was deep and full of what Charlene could tell was regret.

"Six months later I heard she was getting high. I tracked her and MacD down in L.A. and could see for myself that she was heading down the same path as our parents. I begged her to come with me, to come home with me." His voice cracked.

Charlene ached for him. Wrapping her arms around him, she held him tightly.

"That was eight years ago. I haven't spoken to her since. She's been in and out of rehabs. Every time I try to get in touch she pushes me away. I don't know if I'm gonna try again."

"You will," she whispered. "You will because you love her and you want what's best for her. She's sick, Akil. You can't take anything she says seriously."

"I know all that. I try to convince myself of that every day. But it's all so textbook, so predictable. The child following in the parents' footsteps. But I didn't," he said adamantly. "I didn't. I wanted more and I got it."

"Yes, you did. There are more like you, only the statistics don't show the success stories."

"But what if more isn't enough, Charlene? What if everything I obtained isn't enough?"

She didn't know the answer to that, didn't really know what he was asking her. So instead of commenting she just held on to him, reaching up and kissing his lips lightly. "You're enough for me," she said and kissed him again.

His arms wrapped around her. He pulled her on top of him and words were no longer necessary.

He had to be kidding. There was no way they were heading to a shopping mall the day after a hurricane had ravaged the city.

"It's the best time to shop because people whose homes were hit are busy cleaning up. The malls aren't crowded," he'd told her as they climbed in the back of the limousine.

She could relate to what he was saying but thought it might have been a little insensitive. That probably wasn't Akil's intent, just his rationale. He could be very blunt, brutally honest and sometimes a bit unsympathetic, she'd come to realize in the weeks of spending time with him. But after hearing about his childhood, she couldn't really blame him. She didn't show him pity when he talked about his past, didn't mention how sorry she was for the boy who was forced to grow up too soon and for all the love he'd lost on the way. All through her own childhood she'd felt like an outcast, like the Lord surely had dropped her into the wrong family. But for all that her mother wanted to change her and her father working so much he barely knew what was going on in the household and her sister was traveling so much she rarely got to see her, Charlene always knew that she was loved. No matter what, she knew that at least one weekend out of the month she'd be in a room with both her parents and her sister and for at least a few moments they'd be together sharing a smile, a meal, a laugh, making a memory.

It took her a moment to realize Akil was already pulling her in the direction of Saks Fifth Avenue. The sign out front, just between tall looming palm trees, a koi fishpond full of beautiful koi and flowers, read the Bal Harbour Shops. Because shopping wasn't one of her favorite pastimes she couldn't say she'd ever been here. Akil, on the other hand, looked as if he knew his way around this mall and was headed directly where he wanted to be.

Once in the store he looked toward the women's section, to which she'd quickly replied, "This is your shopping spree, not mine."

He only laughed, held her hand a little tighter in his

own and moved to the men's section. He took his time, she thought as she watched him go from rack to rack of jeans. In his mind he probably had an idea of what he wanted and he wasn't going to be pleased until he found it. That's sort of the way he worked in the studio, pushing until the sound was just right. She found she admired that about him.

"Try these on," she heard herself saying as she scooped a pair of pants from the rack and handed them to him.

He looked a little skeptical but reached for them. Taking a look at the size tag he glanced back up at her. "How do you know what size I wear? Have you been sneaking into my closet?" he asked in a tone that was obviously teasing.

Sleeping with him last night had translated to him moving all her stuff from the guest room to his. "You didn't leave me any space to hang my clothes so I had to move some of yours around. And let me say you have just as many clothes as the women I know combined."

He smiled. "I like to look good."

"Just try the pants on."

"Don't try to get me in those skinny jeans I see guys wearing now. That's not going to work with me."

"Yuck, no, I don't think that should work for any man. All these are regular bootcut," she told him, handing him yet another pair of jeans, this time darker than the ones he already had thrown over his arm.

An hour and five pairs of jeans—including the two pairs she'd selected—three dress shirts and a couple of jogging suits later they were headed to the women's department.

"I don't need anything," she said instantly.

"I didn't ask if you did."

"Then I don't want anything."

"I didn't ask you that, either."

She sent him a smoldering look at that remark, but he ignored her and kept moving toward the other side of the store. Where he finally stopped had her both gasping and turning to walk away.

Akil grabbed her by both elbows, turning her back around. "Come on, it's your turn."

"I told you I didn't need anything," she said, hastily looking around. "And I definitely don't need anything from this department."

Heat fused the back of her neck and freckled her cheeks as she stood in the middle of two aisles full of lingerie. From long silky nightgowns to skimpy little teddies to what looked like a bunch of straps and strings arranged neatly on a hanger, this was so out of her element. While she'd enjoyed shopping with Akil for himself, this was a little more personal than she'd ever imagined he'd want to do for or with her.

"I like this." He held up a black nightie that would probably stop along the middle part of her thigh. It wasn't bad-looking, it just wasn't for her.

She shook her head negatively. Akil simply tossed the garment into the shopping bag with the rest of his soon-to-be purchases. "Ooh, and this one is a definite," he was saying.

He'd left her in the first aisle and was now a short distance from her, picking up something else. Charlene raced around to the other aisle to see what he'd picked up this time. "No, Akil. Absolutely not!" she said, her voice elevated a bit. Looking around, she took a step closer to him and reached for the ruby-red sheer item he held.

Of course, he held his arm up higher, keeping the

piece out of her reach. "Are you kidding me? This is hot! I can visualize you in it now."

She made another reach for it but he simply took a step back. "No. No. No. Don't you visualize anything."

But when she looked at him she could tell he was doing just that. His eyes had grown darker and his tongue was stroking his lower lip.

"Akil, I'm not playing."

"C'mon, baby girl. You can see it, too," he said, holding the nightie in front of her.

Reluctantly Charlene looked down. It was sexy, she'd say that much. What she'd seen that was sheer was a jacket held together by one thin silk red string. Beneath it was what looked like a high-waisted one-piece bathing suit. It was strapless and of course red satin, with laces going from the breast cups down right to the crotch.

She swallowed and put a hand to her chest. "I can't visualize it," she said slowly, then turned away.

Coming up behind her, Akil placed a hand on her shoulder. "What's the matter, Charlene? Did I say something wrong?"

She shook her head. "No. It's not you, it's me." Then she chuckled. "That sounds so cliché."

"Actually, it sounds like a lie."

She turned to face him. "Look, Akil, I just don't want you to buy me that because then you'll expect me to wear it."

He nodded. "You're right, I would expect you to wear it. And I know you'll look terrific in it."

"No, I won't."

With a finger to her chin he lifted her face until she was looking directly into his eyes. "You look terrific absolutely naked. Adding this garment can only enhance that beauty. I don't want you to be shy around me or nervous that I won't like how you look. I'm telling you right now that I like everything about you, physical and mental. Okay?"

No, it wasn't okay, she thought with even more flames of embarrassment shooting through her body. Not to mention the instant arousal she always felt whenever he was touching her.

"Baby girl?" he whispered, then leaned forward and kissed the tip of her nose. "Did you hear what I said?" He kissed both of her eyes, her cheeks, then finally her lips.

She nodded. "I heard you."

"Do you believe me?"

And she had to tell the truth. What one man thought of her shouldn't have meant so much. She'd lived in this body with her feelings about it and her acceptance of it for far too long to still rely so heavily on words or opinions. Still, it felt good, it felt right. "Yes, Akil. I believe you."

"Good," he said with one last smacking kiss on her lips. "We're getting this red one and the black one. Now let's see what else we can buy in this store today."

And just like that, their shopping spree continued. As if it were the most natural thing in the world, like they'd been together for months and months, they moved through the mall, laughing and window-shopping, purchasing and laughing some more. It was maybe one of the best times of Akil's life.

He only hoped it could last.

Chapter 14

Mrs. Williamson fixed a spectacular dinner of ham, homemade baked macaroni and cheese, collard greens and apple pie. Charlene ate a full plate with a smile on her face.

Today had been perfect. Spending it entirely with Charlene, there was only one other thing that could top their day.

Music.

After dinner when she'd assumed they'd relax and prepare for bed he fooled her by going straight to the studio.

"You want to work now?" she was asking from behind him. "Aren't you tired?"

He chuckled. "No. And you shouldn't be. We didn't walk that much."

"Oh, yeah, tell that to my aching feet. Well, at least

my stomach's full. But if you don't mind I'll just watch you work for a while."

"Whatever you want, baby girl."

Unable to keep his hands off her for long periods of time, Akil draped an arm over her shoulder as they went through the first door that led down a short hallway to another door. This second door was the soundproof entrance into the studio. Once inside they headed directly to the live room, where Charlene quickly pulled up a chair and sat down.

"Did you take your medicine today?" he asked, eyeing her suspiciously.

"Yes, I did," she replied. "But I didn't get much sleep last night. Remember?"

He nodded. "That's right, you were afraid of the wind and rain. Couldn't sleep."

Just as he'd expected and wanted to see, she smiled. "Yeah, that's exactly what happened."

Today had been a first for him. He sensed it was because of the woman, because of what he knew he was beginning to feel for her. Those feelings unnerved him because he knew they were headed in a direction of uncharted territory. He didn't fall in love with women, didn't allow himself the time or the energy to do so. He had sex, that was natural, a need that required slaking from time to time. Anything beyond that was a hassle and a danger to the man he'd become.

Switching on the power, he pulled up the recording he'd been aching to listen to all day. It was his favorite instrumental. He wanted to listen to it because lyrics had been bubbling around in his head all day long.

"You really like that arrangement, don't you?" Charlene asked from her seat a few feet away from him.

He nodded. "It speaks to me."

"I know what you mean."

And he knew that she did. From the very first time that she'd listened to it he knew she'd felt it.

"She's afraid to give him her love," Charlene began saying.

"But she has so much love to give. He'd be honored to have it."

Charlene began to hum with the music, he suspected because she was so used to the melody by now.

"And after all is said and done you're mine," she sang along with the rhythm that signaled the hook of the song was beginning.

To his own surprise, and he was sure hers, too, Akil joined in. "You belong to me and I belong to you."

The fact that he could sing only startled her for a minute. Most producers were multitalented when it came to music. They could definitely carry a tune and in today's market could most likely flow with the smooth ease of a practiced rapper. The music was in his mind, in his soul, the slick sound of his tenor voice said it reached a part of him that most singers only hoped for.

"You belong to me and I happily belong to you," she sang and closed her eyes, listening as the rhythm slowed again. "When I first met you I didn't believe—didn't want to consider the possibilities. But with the first touch, the first taste I was lost."

The lyrics just flowed and she sang. They were passing the time, letting their combined love of music entertain them for the evening. But when her eyes opened again it was to see Akil staring at her, a pencil in hand and piece of paper in front of him.

"Go on," he prompted when she stopped.

"Oh, no, I was just thinking out loud. I didn't mean—" she stammered.

"It's good. The lyrics are good. She was nervous about loving him in the beginning and then what?"

"She," not her, not Charlene. He wasn't thinking about her when he thought of this song. That was her thought and she sighed. If she weren't such a coward she'd just tell him that each time she heard this melody she thought of nothing but them. From that first night she'd heard it she'd felt his soul and hers in the very beat of the music. Last night they'd made love to this very rhythm in its extended version and then as it was stripped to one instrument at a time. The rhythm of their bodies matched this song from every up-tempo sweep to the straining piano solos.

But Akil didn't seem to know that.

"What about him?" she asked.

For a second he paused, then his head nodded in beat with the music. "Even I wasn't convinced. Something was there but was it true? Could it be what I've always wanted but never really knew existed?"

His voice sent chills down her spine, in a good way, of course. She felt the sincerity and wanted desperately to believe that it was coming from his heart and not just his creative mind.

"Could she be the one for me? Does she know I desperately want her to be?"

With that Charlene's gaze locked with his and the next thing she knew she was standing, moving toward him. Her heart hammered in her chest, her mind screaming questions that her body refused to hear. Her actions were purely emotional, purely physical at this moment, and that's just how she wanted them. To think about what she was doing, what she was risking, might cost her too much.

Cupping Akil's face in her hands, she stared deep

into his eyes and sang with the hook once more, "You belong to me and I belong to you. You belong to me and I happily belong to you."

His hands had snaked up to her hips as she sang, his eyes shifting to that molten color, lust rising in him just as it was in her. But was that all? Not for her, she knew. For Akil, she could only hope.

Lowering her head, she touched her lips to his. Tentatively at first, then with more pressure, more persistence. He obliged, matching her movements and coaxing her tongue to join in the mix. Before long she was straddling him. Her arms wrapped around his neck, his around her back, moving up and down, and they struggled to breathe without breaking the connection of their mouths.

The music in the background was louder than last night but Charlene wasn't really listening. She was feeling, every trickle of heat, every massage of his hands. Her body was on fire with need, a scorching storm building inside waiting, aching for release.

When she knew her lips were swollen from their kisses Akil stood, lifting her in his arms as if she weighed no more than a CD in its case. With one arm he pushed the pencil and paper on the control board aside before sitting her down.

"You belong to me," he sang, his fast-moving fingers going to the buckle of her jeans, pulling them apart and down.

She shimmied out of them, heard the jeans and her shoes fall to the floor. Next went her shirt and her bra. Akil bent forward, kissed each nipple, all the while humming along with the music.

Bracing herself back on her flattened palms, she offered herself to him, totally, completely. He was slow in removing her panties, his lyrics mumbled as he pulled them down her thighs with his teeth.

Charlene was wet and trembling, her desire for Akil quick and potent. With strong hands he grasped her thighs and pushed them apart.

"Could she be the one for me?" his voice sang and her body hummed along.

With one arm extended he touched the tender moist folds of her center, his eyes fastened on hers. His other hand made quick work of his own buckle and he pushed his pants and boxers down his thighs. "Could this belong to me and only me?"

That line shocked her, not just in the words but in the almost falsetto voice he'd used to sing them. At the sound her nipples tingled, her center clenching and juicing more along with his touch.

When his first finger entered her she wanted to scream but bit her bottom lip instead.

"Uh-uh, don't hold it in," he whispered, coming closer so that his thick erection brushed along her inner thigh teasingly. His lips were so close to hers, his warm breath fanned her face. "Nobody can hear you in here, baby girl. If this belongs to me," he said, then traced a heated path from her cheek to her lips and sang, "say my name. Sing your pleasure and say my name."

She could feel the broad head of his sex pressing past her swollen folds and scooted a little closer, eager for him.

"Sing your pleasure," he repeated as just the head pressed forward.

Her body vibrated with anticipation and longing and she inhaled, exhaled.

"Say my name."

And she did, in a long note held in A minor she sang

his name so that there would be no question, no mystery, no denial. She was all his.

As she sang, her voice meshing with his. Akil pushed deeper inside her, feeling his own body convulse with the pleasure. His strokes were slow, measured, but the feel of her lush breasts against his chest even through the material of his shirt was too arousing to keep up that motion. In no time he was thrusting deeply and quickly, loving the sound of their arousal combined with the music and their voices.

Both of them were singing, gyrating, feeling, needing. It was like they were caught up in this funnel of emotion that was spun just for them. And as he felt himself nearing his climax her body shook against his.

Her lyrics changed, slowed until it was if she were just whispering in his ear, her body still shaking from her release. "I think I'm in love with you."

With those words his own release came. In a rush of feeling from his scrotum bursting through his engorged head, he let go. Poured everything he had directly into her.

The words tumbled out, as if they were expected—no, written in the lyrics of the song that Akil now knew belonged to them. "I think I'm in love with you, too."

It was back to business on Monday when Charlene walked into the studio. Akil had gotten up a little earlier, going for a run. He'd whispered in her ear as she continued to sleep in his bed. More and more Charlene was beginning to feel that was exactly where she belonged.

After their heated admissions about possibly being in love with each other she'd expected being together outside the bedroom would be awkward. The exact opposite had occurred. On Sunday Akil had been attentive, open about his past, his feelings, his future plans. It was perfect. So much so she was almost afraid to go back into the studio, to bring more people into their newfound bliss.

"There you go," Jason was saying, dropping an arm over Charlene's shoulders. "How'd you handle the storm?"

She must have looked a little startled at his question because then he said, "The hurricane? I see Viola did no damage to the house. Akil said you mostly had strong rain Friday night and most of Saturday morning. On Thursday you said you didn't like storms."

Oh, yeah, she'd forgotten all about the hurricane. With an inner smile she wondered why. "I did fine. It wasn't as bad as I'd anticipated," she said, trying to keep her gaze from Akil's.

He hadn't looked at her, either. He was at the control board, his fingers moving over the buttons, adjusting the sound, getting everything prepared. He was in business mode, so she assumed she'd better do the same thing.

"Listen, I've got some news. I was waiting until you came so I could tell you both together," Jason said.

Akil did look up then. "What news?"

Jason was rubbing his long fingers together, his caramel-toned skin almost gleaming as he smiled. Whatever it was he had to say must be good. "Seven Nights, you know that new club down in South Beach?" he said to Akil.

"Yeah? What about it?"

"Well, the club's promoter is dating my cousin. I saw him over the weekend at a family gathering and he mentioned they were looking for hot new talent to premiere at the club. Said the crowd on Friday nights is sick. They start packing in around nine, he wants acts to hit the stage around ten, ten-thirty. Like thirty-five grand per night," Jason finished with a slap of his hands together. "What do you say?"

Akil was already looking skeptical. "It's not about the money," he said first.

"I know that, man. It's the exposure. I think she's ready."

Charlene had no idea what club they were talking about but she was focused on Akil, on his reaction to what Jason was saying.

"It would be good exposure. Like a test run," Akil added finally.

Jason was nodding his agreement. "The buzz would already be underway before we even hit Vibe. It's good, Ace. So you want me to call him?"

Akil's gaze finally found hers as he nodded. "Yeah. Call him, tell him we've got a hot new singer that will blow his mind."

"Somebody want to clue me in on what's going on?" Charlene asked, not unnerved by Akil's gaze as much as she was curious.

"You're performing at a club on Friday," he said as simply as if he'd given her the time of day. "Get into the booth so we can go over what you're going to sing."

And just like that the day's work began. Later, Charlene thought, she'd have the meltdown about performing in public, but for right now, all she had to do was sing.

Chapter 15

"Were you busy?" Charlene asked Rachel, the cell phone pressed to her ear as she walked along the terrace.

Jason and Five were still in the studio with Akil remixing one of the tracks they'd finally gotten recorded. It was almost midnight and Akil had come into the booth personally to tell her she was finished for the night.

"You did good," he'd said with a smile. But hadn't touched her, hadn't made a move remotely intimate.

Charlene had tried not to be hurt by the nonaction. She'd been trying all day long. Singing love songs when you're about twelve feet away from the man you love and he's acting like you're just another employee isn't exactly an ideal working condition. Still, the butterflies that seemed to have moved back into her stomach kept her plenty occupied in the meantime.

Her first performance as Charlene Quinn, the singer, the R&B artist. She sighed.

"No. What's up? You don't sound so good."

Taking a seat in one of the high-backed white chairs, she let her muscles relax even though her mind still reeled with all that had gone on in the past few weeks. The fast track to a singing career had been the furthest thing from Charlene's mind, ever. And now here she was. To top it off she was in Miami, where the only people she knew she also worked for. Her friends, her family, were all on the West Coast.

"I'm trying," she said and knew it didn't sound convincing.

"Trying to what? Charlene, just tell me what's wrong."

Now Rachel's voice had hiked up a notch, which meant she was getting worried. Not Charlene's plan.

"I'm singing in a club on Friday. Akil and Jason think I'm ready."

"That's fantastic! Your first performance," she practically yelled and Charlene could tell she was smiling. "So wait, why do you sound like that's a bad thing?"

"Not necessarily a bad thing, but certainly a new thing."

"Well, that's part of being an entertainer. You sing, record the CD then you go out to promote it. That's how it works."

"Excuse me if I'm still trying to acclimate myself to this singing-as-a-career thing. It's been barely a month and I'm already recording my first CD and performing in clubs. That's not how it usually happens."

"But you're not usual," Rachel quipped.

"Gee, thanks." With two fingers Charlene rubbed her temple.

"You know that's not how I meant it. I'm just saying that you should be happy. Like you said, this is not how it usually happens. You've seen for yourself how many singers wish for this their whole lives and still never get it. You should be thankful for your talent and extremely encouraged that Akil and your record label have this type of confidence in you."

Leave it to Rachel to sound so logical. "And I am."

"But?"

"But—" Charlene hesitated, looked up at the indigo sky void of any stars that she could wish on "—I'm scared."

"Of?"

"What if they don't like me? What if I'm not good enough? What if all this was just a dream and I'm going to wake up the minute I step on that stage and all those people staring up at me start to laugh?"

Rachel chuckled. "I swear I've never known anyone who could 'what if' something to death like you."

"Ha-ha, very funny," Charlene quipped, even though Candis often told her the same thing. "You know what I'm trying to say."

"I do," Rachel said with a sigh. "And I get it. I know how you feel about performing in front of people, but, Char, I've got to tell you, for a long time I've thought that was all just in your mind. I mean, take the karaoke bar, for instance. You didn't want to do that but you did. There were about thirty or so people in the audience that night and you got right up there and sang. So good you landed a record deal."

"I did that for you."

"Partly, yes. But more so because you love it. You were born to sing."

Charlene smiled. "That's a movie, Rach."

"Is it?"

"I think so. Or is that *A Star Is Born?*"

"I don't know, you're the one into watching all those old movies. Anyway, what I'm trying to say is once you get on that stage you forget about all those reservations you've nursed since you were a kid. You forget how many people are staring at you and what they may or may not be thinking about your physical looks. You just sing. And when you do people are entranced by your voice."

"So what you're trying to say is don't worry, they're not really looking at me anyway."

"No," Rachel added quickly. "That's not what I'm trying to say. I'm saying that all this stuff about not looking good or not looking like other people is a complex that your mother created and you've nursed. It might be time to let it go, you know."

The words sounded so right. Rachel was honest and she cared. That's why she was her best friend. "I hear you."

"But are you listening to me, Charlene? You're twenty-five years old and in a position that a lot of people would die for. Do you really want to throw it all away because you don't think you look good enough? Because you know you can sang," she said with a giggle and that twang to her voice that always made Charlene laugh.

"I'm listening to you. I always do," she said truthfully. That's why she'd called Rachel first. While Candis was her older sister and Charlene valued her opinion, she and Rachel were not only closer in age, they were closer, period, had more in common. Charlene knew undoubtedly that she could always count on Rachel. That's why her next words came out as smoothly as if she were talking about the weather. "I'm in love with Akil."

"What? Wait a minute, you're confusing me. Weren't we just talking about you being nervous about singing onstage, in front of people? Now you're telling me you're in love with someone? *Akil?* As in your *producer?*"

"Okay. Okay. Slow down, maybe I should have given the conversation change a minute to sink in," Charlene said, unable to help herself from laughing. "Yes. I said I'm in love with Akil, my producer."

"And," Rachel said slowly, "when did you come to that conclusion and what brought you there? What happened?"

"At first he was an ass. I mean, honest and truly, there were days when I felt like knocking him right out."

"Obviously that changed," Rachel said.

"You wanna hear the story or not?"

Rachel chuckled. "Okay, sorry. Go ahead."

"Then he kissed me. And then we had breakfast, lots of breakfasts. You know he doesn't like coffee?"

"Ah, no, I didn't know that."

Of course she didn't, Charlene thought and smiled. She was babbling. She made a concerted effort to stop. "Anyway, we spent some time together and then we slept together and we talked. And we went shopping and we slept together again. And I just figured out that I'm in love with him."

"Okay," Rachel was saying in that slow voice again. "And how does he feel about you?"

"He said he thinks he's in love with me, too."

"Are you happy about that?"

"I think."

"But you're not sure?"

"Where Akil is concerned I can never be too sure."

"Girl, I need to get on a plane and get to Miami. You know I can't leave you on your own for too long."

"Hush, you know I can handle myself." She let out a long sigh. "I just needed to get some things off my chest. But really, I'm doing fine. Actually, I might be excited about performing on Friday if I hadn't gotten the stylist Akil hired fired."

"And how did you do that?"

"By being me," she answered with a chuckle.

"Yeah, right. And I'm sure this person didn't do anything to deserve getting fired. But never you fear, even though I'm across the country you know I've got your back."

"How? What are you going to do, Rachel?"

"Don't worry, I've got this."

"Rachel," Charlene said warningly.

"Oh, I've gotta go, Ethan's here."

"Uh-huh, don't even try it. Ethan is not there. Rachel, what are you going to do?"

"He is here and I have something to talk to him about. Girl, Sofia is having a fit."

"Oh, no. What's going on? I haven't spoken to her but I was going to call her to let her know about the show."

"Don't worry. I'll tell her. But she's still reeling from Uncle Jacob's decision to merge Limelight with A.F.I."

"Wait a minute. A.F.I., Artist's Factory Outlet, your rival talent agency?"

"Yes, that's the one. Apparently my family has a problem with the Jordans, who own A.F.I., or at least the previous generation did. So we're inclined to carry out the feud. Except Uncle Jacob doesn't want that anymore. He wants this merger."

Charlene knew what Rachel was going to say next. "And Sofia isn't trying to hear that."

"Girl, she's livid. You know Limelight is her life. She wanted to take the helm after Uncle Jacob retired. It's always been her dream. And now she feels like he's taking that from her."

"But he's not firing her, right? That would be crazy. Sofia's the best at what she does."

"I agree and so does Uncle Jacob, that's why he's suggesting she and Ramell Jordan become partners. But you know how Sofia is about being the boss."

"I sure do. Not a good situation."

"Not at all. But look, you don't worry about a thing. I'm going to get off this phone, make a quick call and have you set for Friday. Just trust me."

A half hour later when Charlene was stepping out of the shower she had a funny feeling about Rachel's words. But she'd known her forever so she would trust her, this time.

The next day's session was cut short as Akil had some business meetings to attend. Charlene was left to entertain herself in the big house. Mrs. Williamson, of course, was around cooking and cleaning as usual. She'd even seen Nannette as she'd headed out to the terrace, which was quickly becoming her favorite spot.

She didn't know if it was the quiet rustle of the waterfall picturesquely situated toward the end of the pool or the beautiful skyline the back of the house afforded. Against the crystalline blue sky and sparkling sunshine the tips of trees spread into an expanse of deep green. Lower to eye level, palm trees swayed in the warm breeze, creating an almost tropical—without being on an island—feel. She loved it, which was probably due to the fact that she was from California and used to this summerlike scenery all year long.

Nannette had been a darling and purchased all the magazines she'd asked her for. So with a cup of warm tea with honey, Charlene made herself comfortable in one of the lounge chairs and settled in for the afternoon.

She had fashion magazines, which she was sure would have Candis on some of their pages, music and entertainment magazines. What she was looking for she had no clue. Actually, she did, she wanted to know what "the look" now was. Wanted to know if she was remotely close since Serene and her sidekick were now out of the picture.

Akil had come to bed late last night. Though she'd heard him in the shower, felt him climb in bed beside her, reach for her and hold her throughout the night, she hadn't awakened fully and they hadn't talked. This morning Jason was there for breakfast, so again, she didn't have the chance to ask him about the lack of a stylist or her having no clue what she was going to wear on Friday. He'd promised to spend the evening with her as he'd kissed her before leaving this afternoon. He'd seemed a little agitated but she figured maybe he just didn't want to deal with the meeting right now. He hated to be interrupted while working on a CD and since hers was on a fast track, meaning they hoped to at least drop the first single early next year, a day away from recording could really hurt them. The days lost due to the hurricane had been setback enough.

So she settled in, flipping the glossy pages and seeing some things that she could go for. Jill Scott had a nice, real look. She loved the woman's voice and admired her stance to sing only songs with lyrics she'd personally experienced. Her Neo-Soul sound was original and definitely had an audience. And she wasn't wafer thin, either. That made Charlene smile, boosting her ego just a bit.

A picture of the pretty but slim Keri Hilson was on another page, her hair in a longer, feathery style. Charlene liked the color—like a soft bronze, with some blonde highlights. But she was a lighter complexion than Keri Hilson so she wasn't sure how that would look on her. Liya Kebede was in one of the fashion magazines. She was a gorgeous model from Ethiopia. Charlene had met her when she'd traveled to Italy with Candis last year for a photo shoot. She'd enjoyed spending the time with her sister and seeing all the hard work that went into modeling. It definitely wasn't always as glamorous as it looked. Both Liya and Tia St. Claire Donovan—another model whom Candis and Charlene had actually known for a couple of years and who had just a few months ago married the infamous Trent Donovan and given birth to her first son—had complexions just a shade darker than Charlene's. And both of them had eyes that weird shade of hazel and darker brown like she did. So Charlene concentrated on their hair color and their makeup, wondering if any of the tones could work for her.

"I don't need no help. Stop following me, I can find the pool."

She heard a high-pitched voice but didn't think it was exactly female. It was getting louder and she wondered who it could be.

"See, she's right here. I told you I didn't need any help."

Charlene looked up and had to do a double take.

"Following me around like a stalker. Or like I'm gonna steal something. She better recognize."

Not too tall, maybe five-seven, five-ten in the black silver-heeled stilettos he wore. Charlene had to strain her eyes because she could have sworn she was correct in assuming *he*. But…

"Charlene Quinn, girl, I know you betta get up off that chair and give me a hug. Don't make me come over there and yank your behind."

The face definitely looked familiar, caramel-toned, slim, pert lips, assessing eyes. Wait a minute, she began thinking, moving her legs to stand from the chair. Magazines fell to the ground but Charlene was too busy staring to care.

"What? I look good, don't I?"

He struck a pose and Charlene couldn't help but take in his full attire, skinny-legged black jeans, a slim-fit T-shirt tied into a knot just above a flat stomach and dangling navel piercing, black-and-silver bangles dancing up both arms and two diamond studs sparkling from the ears. The hair was a short, sleek asymmetrical bob that even Charlene had to admit was fierce. She thought she recognized him.

"Mark?" she finally gasped, taking a step closer. "Mark Hopkins?"

With a wave of his hand and a jingle of all the bracelets on that wrist, his lips turned and he sucked his teeth. "I'm Mia now," he said and emphasized that change by using both hands to cup his modest breasts.

Her gaze immediately dropped and rested there. "What? Who?"

"That's right, baby. I've got my own now. And you—" he actually reached out and flicked one of Charlene's breasts with one long finger "—you're going to be so jealous when I surpass your girls."

Shaking her head, Charlene was still trying to get a

grasp of this situation. "What are you doing here? And when did you get these? When did you become *this?*" she asked for lack of a better word.

"'This,' as you so rudely put it, has always been me. You know how I used to always hang out with you and Rachel instead of the quote-unquote boys."

He was talking and Charlene couldn't help but recognize how his arm motions and facial expressions seemed a little over-the-top. Then again, this entire person standing in front of her was over-the-top.

"Mark, I mean, Mia," she corrected when one elegantly arched eyebrow on his face raised in question. "I just can't believe it. Does Rachel know? Wait a minute, what are you doing here? How did you know I was in Miami?" Charlene asked suspiciously.

"First, I want my hug," Mia pouted.

"Oh, boy-girl, get over here." Charlene said, grabbing her old friend in a hug. Mark had always been skinny and for a while Charlene had hated him because he ate like a hog and didn't gain an ounce. It felt a little funny hugging him now that he had the unmistakable curve of breasts. "It's been a long time since I've seen you. I see you've changed a lot in that time."

Mark pulled back, waving that hand again. "Girl, I started hormone therapy about nine months ago. I'm preparing for the full gender reassignment."

"A sex change? You're getting a sex change operation?"

"Chile, now you know that's déclassé. Talk like you've been brought up right. What would Mrs. Quinn say if she heard you? It's gender-reassignment surgery."

Yeah, whatever. It was weird in Charlene's book. "Are you sure this is what you want to do?"

He touched those breasts again. "It's a little too late to change my mind."

"Oh." Charlene shrugged. "I guess so. Now answer my question, what are you doing here?"

"Rachel called me last night going on and on about you getting a record deal and performing in a club. The first thing I asked was who was going to do your hair. Because, girl, you know you never get anything good done to your hair. And it's such a shame, you've got such a good grain."

Mark's—Mia's—fingers were already pulling the ponytail holder from her hair. He raked through the length, straightening it so that it lay limply on her shoulders.

"Ump, see, this is what I mean. Such great length and volume. You know people would kill for this kind of hair."

"Yeah, right. People like who?" Charlene snapped.

"People like Lynell Dennison. You remember her? Girl ain't never had more than three strands of hair and they were all nappy as hell."

Charlene laughed so hard at the memory and the way Mark said it she had to sit back down. "You haven't changed a bit. Well, you have, but, you know, you're still just like I remember you."

"I'm only improving the outside, there's no hope for the inside, honey. Now, we have to make you divalicious for Friday."

"What is divalicious?"

"It's a Mia Hopkins original, that's what it is. And when I'm finished with you everyone from here to L.A. will be looking for me to reinvent them, too. Now, come on, let's go shopping."

Charlene didn't even argue, just got up and headed

out the door with Mark—no, Mia. If he wanted to be a she, Charlene wasn't in any position to argue. Wasn't she about to make some changes to her appearance? It was the same and yet different, but she wasn't going to overanalyze the situation. No, today, Charlene Quinn was simply going to go with the flow.

In the mall again. Charlene almost sighed but this trip was full of laughing and chatting just as much as it was shopping. Some of the stuff Mia pulled out was just too off the hook for Charlene to even consider. And then there were the rare pieces that she actually thought she could like.

"Stop being so uptight. You've got good curves, you need to flaunt them," Mia was saying as they walked into yet another store.

Charlene was walking behind him, her hand absently touching the black dresses on the rack in front of her. "Serene and Carlo thought I should stick to empire waists to cover my problem area."

Mia spun around so quick he almost fell on top of her. "What problem area?"

With a sigh, Charlene ran her hands over her midsection. "This one."

Mia clucked his teeth and lifted a finger to tap on Charlene's head. "You mean this one. Because that's the only place you've got a problem."

Charlene swatted his hand away. "Stop playing, this is serious."

"It sure is. Rachel said you were still the same but I couldn't believe it. I figured the years had to have given you some sense."

"Look, Mia, don't cross the line," Charlene warned.

"Oh. Oh." Mia was rolling his neck like a scared chicken, his voice getting louder and louder until two of the salespeople were now staring at them. "I know you're not going to get a backbone with me after you let Ozzie and Harriet tear you down about your size."

"What?" Charlene asked, confused, then sighed. "Lower your voice, we don't need an audience. And who the hell are Ozzie and Harriet?"

"Those two fools that told you all you could wear was empire waists," he said with a roll of his eyes and a toss of his neck, which made his perfectly styled hair sway.

"Serene and Carlo."

"Whatever. The bottom line is they must not have any style themselves, trying to tell you what not to wear."

"Well, it's their job. They're publicists and stylists."

Mia kept right on talking and walking, every now and then picking up a piece, looking at it, then putting it down. "Do they have their own show on a cable network?"

"What? No, they don't have a show."

"Then they don't know what they hell they're talkin' about."

Charlene just shook her head. And Mia said she was still the same. She remembered endless conversations like this during their high school years. Mia fussing about this or that, Rachel either agreeing or arguing with him and Charlene trailing behind the both of them, shaking her head and wondering why she even bothered.

"Okay, now that you've shared your opinion of them, what do you suggest?"

"Oh, now she wants my opinion?" He started looking

around the store, a hand fluttering to his chest. "Little ole me? I'm not a publicist but—"

"Just shut up and tell me what to wear," she said in a huff. He was getting louder and sooner or later one of those salespeople was going to come over and put them out of the store. Then again, she thought looking at Mia, they probably weren't going to come near them no matter how much money they had to spend.

"Humph," was the next reply she received from him before he walked quickly to the back. Along the wall were black cocktail dresses, some simple and some with a little more sparkle.

"Friday is your debut, but it's a sneak peek, right? So you don't want to blast them with everything. You know, don't really give them the whole Charlene Quinn look. Just a glimpse is what'll keep them itching for more."

Charlene agreed.

Mia quickly picked three dresses. "Here, go try these on. Black is simple. And sexy as hell. Go!"

She didn't even bother to argue with him, just took the dresses and moved toward the dressing rooms. When one of the salespeople who had been staring them down since the moment they walked into the store approached with a key she asked, "Could I go in and try these on?"

For a minute the woman looked as if she wanted to say no. A part of Charlene hoped she wouldn't because then she'd have to curse the woman from here right to the courthouse for discrimination. Luckily, she just gave a tight smile and opened the door, ushering Charlene inside.

The first one was a quick no as Charlene's breasts were about to topple over the bodice. The second was just okay, nothing spectacular, according to Mia. The third, thankfully, hit the mark. It was a wraparound with gathers all across the bodice and a straight bottom that looked plain until she walked and her thick thigh peeked through.

"Hotter than hell," Mia had said the moment she walked out of the dressing room. "Simple and sexy. That's what you are, simply sexy."

He chattered on about earrings and shoes and how to style her hair, but Charlene just looked. Standing in the three-way mirror she was able to observe herself at every angle. Black was certainly slimming and she always wore good undergarments. She felt that was the problem with a lot of plus-size women; they refused to spend the money it took to keep their curves looking neat and precise. So there were no hanging rolls, nothing jiggling—that shouldn't be—and nothing about to burst out. She had to admit, this time Mia was right. It was simply sexy.

And Charlene immediately thought of Akil. What would he think of the dress and the way it made her look?

She didn't have ten more minutes to think further before Mia was pushing her back into the dressing room, yelling for her to take that dress off because they had much more shopping to do. Normally she didn't like shopping, but she had enjoyed the other day with Akil. This afternoon, with her old friend who was now sort of a new friend, was shaping up to be just as nice.

Until she heard Mia's loud voice once more.

"Miss, why are you following me around this store like I'm a shoplifter? Do I look like I'm broke?"

All Charlene could do was shake her head. And laugh.

Chapter 16

"Really, Mia. Did you have to threaten that woman at the salon?"

Mia looked totally appalled as they walked into the house after another six hours at the mall. It was after eight in the evening by the time they'd made it back and Charlene was tired. Her feet hurt from walking and her cheeks hurt from laughing so much.

"Are you crazy? That chick did not know me. As cute as I am people should not get it twisted, I will slice and dice anybody who crosses me. Go back to Big Sur and ask that little hoochie who worked in the spa. Tried to put a curly perm in my head." He was using both hands to smooth down his hair, which still wasn't out of place. "Shoot, you know how long it took to get my hair this straight and glossy. I don't know where people get their licenses from."

Charlene was laughing again. "That was like the third time you almost got us arrested."

"Oh, please, I am not afraid of jail."

Charlene dropped her bags as they made their way into the living room. "Well, I am."

"That's because you're uppity. Always have been," he said, waving his hands again and plopping down into the puffy white leather lounge. "Just because your daddy made all that money in movies and TV, you thought you were privileged."

Charlene feigned indignance. "I was."

"Honeychile, you were not. You were the second born and you weren't the model. You were just like me—close but no cigar."

"Shut up!" she said, tossing one of the colored pillows from the couch toward his head. "Your mother acted in just as many movies as my father produced and won just as many awards. And your daddy wasn't any slouch, either, with all the oil money he'd inherited. You're just as uppity as I am."

"But we weren't talking about me. We were talking about—oh…my…Lord." Mia sat up in the chair, staring off at something.

"What?" Charlene asked, following the direction of his gaze.

"Who is that? He is some kind of fine." Mia was getting up out of the chair, smoothing down her shirt and pushing up her breasts.

In the hallway Akil and Jason were talking. It looked as if Jason were leaving for the night.

"Oh, Akil," she called as she started walking toward them.

They both stopped talking and met her halfway. "Hey,

you're back," Akil said, his smile making her warm all over.

"We thought you'd gotten lost. Ace here was about to call out the search posse."

"It wasn't like that," Akil said, looking a little awkward at Jason's words. "I was just wondering where you were."

"I should have left a note. It just happened so quick. Mia showed up and we just headed out to the mall, didn't think about anything else."

"Mia?" Akil asked.

Charlene turned, grabbed Mia's arm and pulled him forward. "My old friend from L.A., Mia Hopkins. Rachel couldn't come so she sent Mia out to help me get ready for Friday's show. That's where we've been, out shopping for my outfit."

Akil barely looked at Mia. "You got your hair done?" he asked.

She smiled and turned to the side and back. "I did. Do you like it?"

"It's nice," Jason said. "Sassy."

"They cut a few inches and feathered it a bit on the ends. I think it's sexy. She needed a little oomph," Mia spoke up.

Akil cut his eyes at him. "This was your idea?"

Mia poked her hormone-enhanced breasts out farther. "Of course. Do you like?"

Akil couldn't tell if she was asking if he liked Charlene's hair or Mia's breasts. Or seeing as she had an Adam's apple the size of a golf ball, he should probably say "his" breasts.

"I liked her before," was Akil's immediate reply. "But this is nice, soft. It fits you."

"I know it does. When I set out to make someone over

that's what I do. And nobody knows Charlene like I do, so I know what's best for her," Mia was saying, moving so that she now stood closer to Akil.

Behind him he heard Jason stifle a chuckle.

"Have you had dinner?" Akil asked Charlene.

"We ate at the mall."

"Yes, we did. But if you'd like to go out for a night-cap?" Mia left the rest to linger in the air.

Akil was about to speak when Charlene grabbed Mia by the elbow. "Enough. It's not even that type of party so move along."

Mia shook his head, looking at her over his shoulder. "I was wondering how long it was going to take you to speak up. If I've told you once I've told you a thousand times—if it's yours stake your claim and make it known."

Turning back to Akil, he said, "Hurt her and I'll bust your kneecaps. Good night."

He walked past Jason, blowing a kiss in his direction. Akil didn't know what to say as they all watched the slim hips sashay out the front door.

However, as soon as the door was closed Jason let out a thunderous laugh that had Charlene following suit. Akil was not feeling the joke.

Actually, he wasn't feeling anything but paranoid right about now. He'd received another phone call, this time with a message. No, he knew this was no laughing matter.

This was it.

Charlene took one last look in the mirror. She and Mia had changed their minds several times in the last few days about what she was actually going to wear. But tonight was the night. The dress she wore was *the* one. And "the look" was all hers.

Her hair was flawless, flipped and feathered to fall softly around her face. Her natural brown color had been lightened just a bit with bronze highlights. Mia swore by MAC cosmetics, so he'd used the Shimpagne Mineralize Skinfinish. The Play on Plums eye finish was a great accent, giving her eyes a bronze/peachy/pink look, and Roman Holiday Dazzleglass gave her lips just enough tinted shine she was sure would last the entire night. Never had Charlene seen her own face look so classically pretty.

The dress was simple and sexy, just "the look" she and Mia had decided would be her signature. A rich black sheath, modern square neck, cap sleeves and slim skirt was the simple. As for the sexy, the seven-inch split up the left leg played the part perfectly. Leopard-print sandals gave that little splash of "wow."

"You're gorgeous."

His voice was deep and sounded solemn as Charlene turned to face Akil. She hadn't known he'd come back upstairs into the room. He was dressed an hour ago and had gone downstairs to talk to Jason. All day he'd been with her, not talking about the show or her performance or the song or anything musical. She had laughed until her sides hurt, him right along with her. The afternoon had been relaxing and comfortable and made her think of their future together.

Akil never talked about their future as a couple. Actually, he never talked about them as a couple. He talked about the CD and how well he thought it would be received. He talked about other music he had in mind for her, appearances, et cetera. But never did he mention them maybe taking a trip together or just going out to dinner together as a couple. She was starting to wonder if this whole thing between them would be one of those celebrity secrets. The press could catch a shot of them together but if asked neither of them would comment, sort of like some popular celebrities were doing right now. People knew they were together but neither of them was actually admitting it. That wasn't something she wanted, wasn't a relationship she thought she could live with. While she had never wanted to be in the spotlight, never wanted to be in the tabloids for any reason, she also didn't want to feel like she was a secret.

"Thanks," she said finally, her hands moving nervously down the front of her dress.

"Don't fidget. You look great just standing there." He took a few steps closer until she could smell his cologne.

"You look really good, too." This was the first time she'd seen Akil dressed up in person. She'd seen pictures in magazines of him at award shows or other clubs, but face-to-face was a whole different story.

The black slacks and matching jacket were Ralph Lauren. His shirt had been delivered while they were watching movies earlier that day. The name on the box was Ace and she'd asked him about the unknown designer. He'd only smiled and said, "You're looking at him."

Now she had the chance to take in the entire ensemble—the wide-collared black shirt with what looked like a paisley print but was actually an array of microphones and long swirling cords in a pale gray color, black slacks and a single-breasted sports coat, with shined-to-perfection gray alligator-and-crocodile-print leather wingtips.

Even though he wore all black his dark complexion

seemed to bask in the colors. His close-cropped hair sported rows of deep soft waves and his eyes held a sort of anticipation she'd never seen before. Her heart flip-flopped wildly in her chest just looking at him.

"I have something for you."

"What? Why?" She was already nervous. The fact that he'd approached her with a hand behind his back and a somber expression wasn't working well to calm her down. She didn't want a gift, not from Akil. That would only add to the confusion she was already feeling about their relationship, which would only add to the anxiety she was feeling about singing at the club tonight, which would undoubtedly increase her chances of having a coronary right there on stage.

Dang, Charlene, can you be any more dramatic? She could almost hear Rachel, Candis and Mia all joined in together. *Okay, just calm down,* she told herself and took a steady breath.

"It's just a little something that I want you to have."

"For tonight?" Her voice squeaked a little with the question. She hadn't eaten a big lunch. Hot tea with honey had been her choice of drink, along with her daily eight glasses of water. So right about now she felt like the bathroom was going to be her second best friend this evening. But her voice would be flawless and that was all that really counted.

The left corner of his mouth lifted upward in a small smile. With his right hand he gripped her wrist and pulled it down to her side so she'd have no choice but to stop clasping and unclasping her fingers. "No. Not just for tonight," he said.

His left arm moved from around his back and he put the telltale blue box in front of her. "Just for you."

Now this was totally unfair. How was she supposed

to accept a gift—from Tiffany's, no less—and not feel shaky? It was a medium-size box so she was sure it wasn't a ring. What she wasn't so sure of was why she even had the flicker of thought that it might be one. She was driving herself crazy with all these questions and no answers, which was the last thing she needed tonight. So with a nervous smile she resigned herself to simply deal with whatever it was and move on.

With one hand she took the box from him. With the other she removed the white bow and flipped the lid. Inside her heart all but stopped but on the outside she made a valiant effort to remain calm. Her slightly shaking fingers lifted the wide sterling silver bracelet with round diamonds marching in one single-file line across the width. "It's beautiful. Thank you, Akil," she managed to say without blubbering.

Akil took the box, put it down on the table near them, then slipped the bracelet from her fingers, unclasped it and put it on her right wrist. "You're very welcome."

His arms slipped slowly around her waist as he pulled her closer to him. It felt good to be in his arms. *Safe,* she thought all of a sudden. "You're going to be great tonight," he said, gazing into her eyes.

She nodded as a response.

"Trust yourself. Trust your voice."

She was nodding again then stopped because she felt like a mute. "I will."

"I love you," he said simply and kissed her lips lightly.

All the doubts, all the questions, all the reservations fell from her and she sighed in his arms. "I love you, too."

* * *

They'd come in a back door and she was taken directly to a dressing room. For a few minutes she was in there alone. Then Jason came in with a pep talk that left her laughing instead of worrying. She didn't see Akil again until she stepped out of the room to walk down the narrow hallway that would lead to the stage. Behind him was Jax and in front of them was Jason and Steve. He took her hand immediately.

Gripping her fingers tightly, he gave them a little shake. "Let's do this."

She smiled. "Let's do it."

A stage tech guided her onto the stage with its dark curtain drawn. Butterflies did more than dance in her stomach; it was like they were having some kind of festival complete with dancing and singing of their own. But her mind fought hard to calm them. She focused on the song, on feeling the lyrics, on making the audience feel the lyrics.

She barely heard her name, really didn't register the tentative applause. But the rustle of the curtain opening jolted her. Jason's directions from yesterday when they did a dry run of the performance replayed in her mind.

Stand still. Wait for the music, the first thumps of bass.

She heard it and her heart beat just a little faster.

The spotlight will go up, he told her. It will move across the stage as if it's searching for you. Wait until it finds you. She waited. Felt the heat of the light, saw the brilliant brightness in her eyes.

She took one step, then two. Then she leaned forward toward the mic and belted the first line of the song.

It was slow, almost as if she were conversationally talking.

"Never like this before. No, never like this. I never loved like this. Never kissed like this. Never felt like this before."

Then the tempo picked up and she sang like she'd never sung before. Like nobody was there, it was just her and the band in the studio. The notes appeared in her mind, she could almost see the song sheet she'd practiced from on so many days. And she just sang.

Everybody was on their feet clapping and whistling as Charlene made her way off the stage. She'd been a hit. She looked absolutely beautiful and he'd never loved anyone more.

With his chest swelling with more emotion than he thought he could handle, he was making his way across the room, trying to get to the backstage door so he could see Charlene. A hand on his arm held him back.

Akil turned to see who'd stopped him and felt waves of dread clogging the air instead. With a nod of his head the guy who had been calling Akil, making outrageous demands and just recently very serious threats signaled they move toward a door near the restrooms. Akil followed him because there was no use making a scene. This was Charlene's night and there were bouncers all over this place. Not to mention Jax and Steve. If he did what he truly felt and knocked this dude the hell out there would surely be a huge fight, one that would definitely make it into every tabloid first thing tomorrow morning.

So he had to keep his cool. It was taking great effort but he did so, following the familiar face until they were closed in the small room alone.

"Well, well, well. Akil Hutton, superproducer," he drawled, a smirk spreading quickly over his face.

"T. K. Dupree," Akil said tightly as he turned, standing with his feet slightly spread, ready for anything.

"You look good, brotha. Glad to see you've been living well. Then again, I already knew that was the case."

"Let's cut the bull. I don't know why you wasted your time coming here. I told you on the phone how I felt about your little ultimatum."

T. K. Dupree, a six-foot-tall, half Puerto Rican, half African American man with short hair and two gold teeth stood in front of him. They were of similar build and similar backgrounds. T.K.'s mother, Rosita, spent many nights at Akil's house. Which meant T.K., also known as Thomas Keith after his father, spent many nights in the lower bunk in Akil's bedroom.

"And I told you I'm not stopping until I get what I want. You've come a long way, brotha. It's time you shared the wealth." T.K.'s hand moved to his waistband, where he no doubt had stashed his piece. Even though Akil had been out of the game for a long time, he still recognized the signs.

"Then you should have worked for it!" Akil spat. "You're a little too old to be a stick-up boy now, T.K."

T.K. just laughed. "You're right. I have outgrown sticking people up for five and ten dollars or whatever those poor junkies had in their pockets. I'm on to bigger and better gigs now. You should know what I mean."

"I know I'm not giving you a dime," Akil said, taking a step back and lifting his arms in the air. "So if shooting me is your final call, do your thing."

"Nah," T.K. said, stepping closer to Akil. "That's

too easy. But I am going to give you one more chance. One million or the whole world finds out that the superproducer has a super secret, one that could land his ass in jail." He was about to walk away but as if he was having an afterthought he looked Akil directly in the eye. "And by the way, your new act, she's a hottie. Wonder what she'd say if—"

Akil reacted instantly, grabbing a handful of T.K.'s shirt and pushing him back until he slammed into the wall. "Don't even think about her. Don't say her name. Don't look her way. Or I swear, T.K., all that we've been through, all that we've seen together will seem like a day in the park compared to what I'll do to you."

Again T.K. laughed. "You know what to do, Akil." He pulled out of Akil's grip. "So do it."

Chapter 17

Now they were back to the silent treatment. For about fifteen minutes during the drive back to the house Charlene wondered why she even bothered. After all they'd shared Akil still had his moments.

The difference now was that she felt somehow compelled to dig deeper, to figure out what was really bothering him. Her performance had been a hit, Akil had said so himself. On top of that, Jason had said so, as had the applauding crowd. Hell, the manager wanted her to come back next Friday night. Akil quickly axed that offer, telling him he'd see her again after the CD release. The guy hadn't looked thrilled but he wasn't about to cross Akil. Just the promise that Akil would bring her back to perform seemed to be enough.

Everything had been going along perfectly until she'd gone to dance with Jason. When they'd come back to the table Akil looked as if he were about to overturn

the table and everything on it. His eyes had gone
dark and dangerous-looking, his shoulders were set,
tension rolling off in thick heavy waves. She'd known
the moment she stepped up to him that something had
happened. She wondered if it had been another one of
those phone calls.

They were about five minutes away from the house
when Charlene started to get angry. With all they'd
shared why couldn't Akil share this with her? Why
couldn't he tell her what had happened to upset him?
Why did she even bother?

The answer to that last question was the simplest one.
She was in love with him.

Whether or not that was an intelligent decision on
her part didn't really matter—it just was.

Cliff brought the car to a stop. Akil didn't even wait
for him to come back and open the door for him, just
jumped out. With a sigh Charlene slid across the seat
and stepped out herself. Mild shock registered as Akil
was still standing by the door waiting for her. His hand
on the small of her back was comforting as they walked
into the house together.

They headed straight for the stairs. Behind her
Charlene could hear the beeps of the security system
being deactivated and activated again. Jax and Steve
were Akil's personal security detail so they'd stayed
with him at all times. At the club there had been four
more guys working security but they'd pretty much
escorted them inside, then watched the doors and she
presumed the car. Jax and Steve were the only two who
stayed with them all the time.

In the club tonight he'd been her producer. In the
studio he was the same. Only at night or when they were
alone did it appear they were more. She sensed that Jason

knew they were sleeping together and of course Jax and Steve knew and most likely his household staff. But nobody on the outside knew. Not even Sofia or Candis. With a start she wondered what they'd think. Would they approve? That, coupled with Akil's mood, had her turning in the opposite direction, heading toward the bedroom that had originally been assigned to her upon arriving in Miami.

Akil had been walking right behind her, his hand on her back, but when she veered away, he didn't follow. And he didn't try to stop her. With hurried footsteps she made her way into the other bedroom, closed the door and fell back against it, stifling a moan.

How could this be happening? How could she have come so far professionally and taken such a giant step backward personally? Never in her life had she allowed a man any type of power over her.

Until Akil.

He'd changed what she'd come to expect from a man, changed what she allowed herself to feel. He told her she was beautiful, that she was worth so much more than the label people around her wanted to slap on her. Things she'd tried to act like she believed on the outside, but had still haunted her on the inside. He'd pulled away the inner blinders and taught her how to feel emotion, passion, to revel in them both.

And yet she wasn't good enough to be allowed to do the same for him. There was something he was holding back, she felt it at times when they were together. He'd told her about his past, shared the emotional scars left by his parents' untimely and unnecessary deaths and his sister's traitorous departure. He shared his body with her unconditionally. But there was something else he was holding back. She knew it as surely as she knew her name.

The question was, what was she going to do about it?

Tonight wasn't the night to answer those questions. She shouldn't have to relinquish the joy of her success to the pain of his secrets. She wanted to call Rachel to tell her how things had gone but it was too late. Nearly three in the morning in Miami was just after midnight in L.A. She wouldn't disturb her by calling at this time, she'd wait until morning.

Stripping off her clothes, remembering how so many eyes had been on her tonight appreciating the way she looked, made her smile. Mia had done a fantastic job with her makeover, although she refused to call it that. Mia's exact words were "I'm simply providing the right accessories to accentuate God's given beauty." That had made her feel good, special, so she decided to hold on to that thought as she headed for the small bathroom and shower.

Staying in Akil's master suite was definitely different than being in this guest room. His shower alone was the size of this entire bathroom, but she wouldn't allow herself those thoughts a second longer. Stepping inside the stall, she turned on the spray of water, adjusting its temperature until the heated drops tingled as they hit her skin. Closing her eyes, she tilted her head and concentrated on the heat, the soothing rivulets of water washing over her. The day and evening's tensions rolled from her with the waves of water, falling to the floor and swirling down the drain. Mental signals moved throughout her body, to each tired or strained muscle so that her focus was on calm, serenity.

She was so engrossed in relaxing herself she hadn't

heard the door open, hadn't felt the quick blast of cool air as Akil stepped into the shower stall with her.

Blood pounded at his temples as he remembered what had transpired at the club. T.K. was in Miami and was following his usual M.O. Everybody owed him something, money, opportunity, his very presence meant he should be important, known, recognized. Akil knew all this, remembered it from their time spent growing up. He hadn't liked it then and despised it even more now. This was a grown man, two years shy of being forty, and he was still living under the same BS philosophy of not working for anything but bullying his way to each and every meal. It was sickening and had Akil so angry that he'd almost punched his old friend right there in the middle of the club, on Charlene's big night.

He felt like scum for even having the thought and hadn't shaken the mood by the time she made it back to the table. He knew she saw the change in him and that only angered him more. The last thing he wanted to do was ruin this moment for her. Damn T.K. for showing up and damn him for falling right back into that old mentality that he needed to get rid of T.K. for good. That he should have done it a long time ago. Just the thought made him feel ashamed, evil, demented. It was part of what he'd run away from years and years ago, part of what he'd prayed would stay in his past. But sometimes—Akil knew this better than a lot of other people he associated with—sometimes, God didn't answer all prayers.

The look in Charlene's eyes as she watched him for the duration of the night had almost destroyed him. The mixture of pity, misunderstanding, question, anger, it all tore through him like a jagged-edged knife. He hadn't known what to say, how to shake the mood, how to fix things with her. The ride home had been tense and uncomfortable for them both. He'd fooled himself into believing they'd get home—his home, funny how he'd begun to think of it as theirs—go to bed and wake up to sunshine and a better day tomorrow.

She'd walked away from him.

He deserved it, he knew, but it stung just the same. And tonight of all nights he couldn't stomach another woman he loved walking out of his life.

So he'd come to her. Not knowing how to do anything else but what he was doing now. Reaching out, wrapping his arms around her waist and pulling her back against his naked body. For one brief second she was startled, then she settled a bit, her body stiff against his.

"I'm sorry, baby girl," he said, burying his face against the softness of her neck. "It seems like I'm always apologizing to you."

She didn't speak.

"I'm trying so hard to be the man you desire. Help me, please."

Her head lay back against his shoulder, one of her water-slick hands reaching up to cup the back of his head. At her touch every tense muscle in his body relaxed, every bad memory of the evening and his life before vanished. There was only the here and now. There was only Charlene.

He kissed her neck, his tongue mixing with the warm water along her silken skin. His hands moved upward, gripping her breasts and squeezing. Against her soft bottom his sex jutted and strained against the condom he'd donned before entering the bathroom. He needed to be inside of her, to feel her completely surrounding him. He needed that like he needed his next breath.

And she knew it.

Covering his hands with her own, they pushed her breasts together, massaged, toyed with puckered nipples and moaned with delight. His mind was a thick haze of desire, like music if sound could be seen and not heard. One of her hands slipped down and back until her deft fingers were wrapping around his thick arousal. He gasped, stroked his tongue over her shoulder, then nipped lightly. Without preamble she guided him between her cheeks, into the dewy haven that he sought. With a ragged moan he slid into her like a moth to a flame, a key to a lock, a player into home base. He was there, safe, finally.

Lifting her hands, he flattened them on the wet tiles in front of them, gripped her hips and pushed deep inside her. Her head fell forward as she moaned, her body shaking with every stroke and retreat.

They didn't speak. Didn't need to because their bodies were totally in sync with their minds. She knew what he needed. He knew what he wanted. The hows and whys didn't really matter at this point.

She bucked against him, pressing her plump bottom into his groin, her sweet walls clasping his erection like a glove. He pulled out and slipped back in, loving the slick heat, the tight and precise fit as if she were made specifically for him.

In and out. Out and in. The timeless motion seemed to go on forever. Until her thighs began to quake, her arms shaking as they were extending above her head. His spine tingled, his scrotum tight and heavy with anticipated release. He closed his eyes, let the swirling vortex of pleasure engulf him. Two powerful strokes later and his release soared through his system, halting in the condom, yet connecting them on a higher, more emotional plane.

For endless moments he held her right there, against the tiles, the water growing tepid. Pulling back only enough so that he was not embedded inside her anymore but their bodies were still pressed tight, he whispered over and over again, "I love you, baby girl. Love you. Love you. Love you."

It had been a week since Charlene's performance at the club and Akil hadn't heard from T.K. He wanted to believe that was a good sign, but knew differently.

In addition to money, T.K. wanted a job at Playascape, something high-profile, he'd told Akil. He wanted to keep his money rolling in. And he expected Akil to oblige. Just like that he expected Akil to give part of what he'd worked for to a man who was determined to do anything with his life but work.

He and T.K. had grown up together, had been through some really tough times, had seen some pretty brutal things. They should have been as close as blood brothers. Instead they appeared to occupy space on two different planets. Akil's answer to their childhood struggle had been to study, to find a goal and work hard toward it.

T.K.'s mind-set was that he was owed by any and everyone, especially those who knew him best and had something. He'd grown up hating the black cop who'd picked his mother up for prostitution yet had her sleep with him for free to keep from going to jail. He hated that his mother had gotten pregnant with him that night in the back of the police cruiser and that she'd spent every day and night after that getting high and continuing to sell her body. Because that jackass cop hadn't looked at her again after throwing her limp body out of his car. For years he'd rolled through their neighborhood arresting some drug dealers, stealing from others, threatening the users and their kids. He knew who T.K. was, found out the first time he arrested him when T.K. was eleven years old. "You ain't nothing, just like your dirty-ass mother," he'd said, then opened the back door to the cruiser and kicked T.K. out after he'd driven him far from the city into Harford County and stripped him of all his clothes. A county cop had brought T.K. home that night but didn't believe his story. Rosita had smacked T.K. so hard when he told her, his bottom lip bled for hours. From that point on T.K. had sworn to kill Officer Thomas Keith Dupree, Sr.

The year they turned eighteen Officer Dupree's body was found in an old crack house two blocks from where Akil and his family lived. He'd been stripped of all his clothes and shot at close range in the head. His killer was never found.

But Akil knew who it was.

He had a secret on T.K. just like the one T.K. had on him. Only nobody would care about a half-assed drug dealer shooting a crooked cop almost eighteen years ago. However, the deeds of a famous music producer making more money than a lot of white men in the country would be made an example of if his past were ever revealed.

The deal he'd just worked out with Sony Electronics for a line of studio equipment would most certainly disappear. Ace, his new clothing line, would never make it to Fashion Week. And his artists, they would suffer, as well. The bad publicity would surely attack their sales.

Then there was Charlene.

He stood to lose the most with her. He loved her, had admitted that to himself and to her. He'd never thought he'd have these feelings for a woman, especially not a woman in the industry—his mother and sister had really jaded him in that area. He wanted to be with her, wanted her to want to be with him.

If T.K. talked that would all change.

But he couldn't, *would not,* give in to blackmail. It went against everything he'd ever believed, ever fought for. He wouldn't be used by anyone, ever again.

"I'm ready," Charlene said as she entered the living room. "Are you okay, Akil?"

"I am now," he greeted her with a smile and a hug. With her in his arms, in his life, he was more than okay. He was perfect and he intended to keep it that way.

Chapter 18

Cine Citta Cafe was one of the trendy restaurants in the Miami Beach area. Akil said he liked the food here and the low-key atmosphere.

"This is nice," Charlene was saying as she opened up her menu. It was their first real date and she was excited. Cliff had driven them but he'd made Jax and Steve follow in another car. There had been a lot of whispering between Akil and Jax before he'd finally gotten in the car and she desperately wanted to ask what was going on but didn't want to spoil the evening.

Now they were seated and about to order and although he was sitting right across from her Charlene still felt like he was miles away. Deciding that enough was enough, she put her menu down. "Akil, what's going on?"

He looked at her strangely. "What? I'm looking at the menu to see what I want."

"You know that's not what I mean. You've been acting weird for a couple of days now. Actually, since the night at the club. What is it? Did I do something wrong?"

"No. No." His answer was quick. He reached a hand across the table to take hers. "You were great. The audience really loved you and the owner wants you to come back again. 'Never Before Like This' is definitely going to be the first single we release. The sound was just right and you looked fantastic up there."

And he was dancing around the real subject like Usher danced around on stage.

"Great. Now tell me what's going on with you. Not the producer. Not the songs on the CD or how I looked. I want to know what's bothering you."

He sighed heavily, released her hand and resumed looking at the menu. "Nothing's bothering me. I'm fine."

"You're not fine," she snapped. "You bounce from happy to sad to mad in ten minutes flat. I'd venture to say you might be bipolar but I don't think it's a chemical imbalance causing your mood swings. I think something is going on, something you don't want to talk to me about." He didn't say anything and she felt like she was losing this battle.

"Jason's worried about you, too. He says you're not focused and that's not like you. I tend to believe him."

Akil slammed the menu on the table. "So you and Jason have been cozying up talking about me?"

"No. Me and Jason care about you and we're concerned. If you gave a damn about us you wouldn't keep us in the dark about whatever it is that's bothering you."

"Don't do that," he said slowly, his dark eyes burning

into hers. "You know how I feel about you, Charlene. Don't use it like that."

"I'm not using anything, Akil. I'm just trying to understand you. Ever since I met you you've been hot and cold, either toward me or just in general. I don't know how to take you from one minute to the next. It's crazy."

"So you want to leave, is that what you're saying?"

Well, where had that come from? This entire conversation was going in a direction Charlene hadn't anticipated and wasn't sure she could handle. But she'd come this far, she wasn't about to back down now.

"I love you, Akil. I came out here to make an album, not to fall in love. But I did and I'm okay with that. I enjoy being with you and working with you. But I feel like you're holding something back from me."

"I'm not seeing someone else, if that's what you think. I'd never do that."

"I didn't think it was another woman. But I know it's something. Something that's keeping you from being with me completely. I don't know what it is and that scares me."

"Don't," he said, reaching for both her hands this time. "You don't ever have to be afraid of me, Charlene. I would never hurt you."

"Well, isn't this cozy."

Akil froze the minute he heard the voice.

"Superproducer Akil Hutton and his new singer, Ms. Charlene Quinn." T.K. was pulling up a chair, sitting down between Akil and Charlene. "Or should I say Akil Hutton and his new honey having a nice romantic dinner? Yeah, that would be a better headline, don't you think, Akil?"

Charlene was looking from him to T.K. and back to

him again. He released her hands and sat back in his chair. "What are you doing here?"

"Come on, man. Is that any way to introduce me to your lady friend?" He extended his hand to Charlene. "I'm T.K., an old friend of Akil's. Actually, we're more like brothers. I'm sure he's told you about me."

Shaking his hand, Charlene looked questioningly at Akil. "No, I'm sorry he didn't. You said you're old friends?"

Akil knew she was remembering back to that night in the pool house when he'd gotten that call and told her it was from an old friend. One of the things he loved about Charlene in the studio was that she was a quick study, she picked up the notes and rhythm after he'd gone over it one time. He could see that she was that way with every aspect of her life.

"Hell, yeah. We go way back. I mean we used to share bunk beds, that's how far back we go."

"That was a long time ago," Akil said tightly. "Why don't you get going, T.K.? You and I can hook up later."

T.K. was shaking his head. "Nah, I'm hungry. You haven't ordered yet, right? So let me get the menu."

"No!" Akil said quickly.

"It's okay," Charlene stated. "I don't mind having company for dinner, Akil."

"Well, I do."

"But we aim to please our women," T.K. said with a wicked gleam in his eyes.

Akil sighed and out of the corner of his eye saw Jax making his way to the table. He held up a hand, halting his bodyguard's approach. He could handle T.K. himself. He just needed to get him away from Charlene.

"How about we go outside and talk," Akil offered.

T.K. picked up a glass of water, drinking slowly. "No, thanks. We tried that and it didn't work. I figure it's time for phase two."

"T.K.," Akil warned.

Charlene put her napkin on the table. "Akil, what's going on?"

Her question echoed in his head, replaying as if she'd been asking him that for hours, days, weeks since they met. "Nothing. I'll take care of it," was his reply but he didn't know if he believed it.

"I hoped you would," T.K. said. "This place doesn't have any red meat, did you know that?" He acted as if he were engrossed in the menu.

Akil pushed back in his chair and stood. "Let's go outside, T.K."

"No," T.K. said simply, letting the menu drop to the table. "Let's not. I have other things to do so I'll make this quick." He looked up at Akil. "You can stand or sit, suit yourself."

"T.K." His voice was low, warning.

"So, Charlene, you're sleeping with Akil here? I guess you could do worse."

"What?" Charlene gasped.

Akil reached for T.K.'s arm and pulled him up. "Don't do this."

T.K. laughed. "Oh, now you're taking me seriously. Too late, bro. What's the matter? You were Mr. Tough Guy at the club the other night, standing me down, even threatening me not to go near your little lady."

"You were at the club last week?" Charlene asked, confusion clear in her voice.

Akil waved his other arm and signaled for Jax to come over; this was getting out of hand. Jax was at the table in seconds. "Get her out of here," he told him.

"You want her to leave before I tell her the news?" T.K. drawled.

Charlene had just pulled her arm from Jax's grip. "What news?"

"I knew he wouldn't tell you. The FBI, they're looking for him."

"I'm gonna kill you," Akil said through clenched teeth.

"Ah, there you go with those threats again. You know I'm scared one day he's really going to go through with it. It's said after a killer makes his first kill the others are like a walk in the park."

Everything around him froze. Jax didn't move. T.K. kept that stupid grin on his face. And Charlene's gaze fell on him, confused, hurt, still.

"A killer," she barely whispered the word.

"Yeah," T.K. lowered his tone to a whisper. "Akil killed his mother—that's why he had to leave Baltimore. And since she was a federal snitch and the Feds just got new info on her killer, they're looking for your boy here. You should probably distance yourself from him now. He'll kill your career." T.K. chuckled. "No pun intended."

"What…" She tried to swallow but her throat was dry, her tongue like a blob of cotton. "What's he talking about, Akil?" She wanted, no, desperately needed to hear a heated denial. Any minute now Akil was going to punch this man for lying. Then they would go home and Akil would explain it all.

"Akil?" she heard herself saying again.

But he wasn't speaking. Actually he looked like he couldn't speak. He looked from her to T.K. and his eyes gleamed. That's what she'd always seen in them, a lining of hate, a fierce violence just brimming under the surface.

Could that violence lead to killing? Did he kill his mother?

The room felt like it was spinning. Her legs began to buckle and Jax's strong arms around her waist were the closest thing to reality she could feel. "Tell me what's going on, Akil." She'd spoken again, a repeat of the question she'd been asking him all evening. "Tell me."

"I'll tell you," T.K. offered. "Betty was a junkie, strung out on that crack and heroin, whatever she could get her hands on. Everybody knew it and nobody cared. Especially not her do-gooder son, the one with his head always stuck in a book. So when she got some bad dope and lay in an alley dying, he looked down on her and left her there. Just walked away and let her die. Ain't that right, Akil?"

Charlene felt like she was choking. Her chest pounded, words died in her throat and she gasped for air. Akil was at her side quickly.

"Baby, just let Jax take you home. I'll explain it all when I get there. Just go home, baby. Please."

His voice was deep, flushed with anger as he whispered in her ear.

"No," she responded weakly. "Tell me now. Tell me right now! Did you do this?"

"Yeah, tell her right now, Akil. Tell her how I stood in that alley with you, watched you leave Betty to die in her own urine and filth. Tell her how when you got to the end of the alley you broke out into a run, leaving me behind." T.K. sat down. "Tell her." He laughed.

Jax hit him then, watched as he fell right off the chair onto the floor. T.K. got up, wiping the blood from his nose. "Now I'm gonna have to sue. Pity." He grabbed a napkin from the table. "You know where to find me, Akil. She was phase two. Don't make me go to the next phase. I promise you'll like it even less."

Akil was still pressed to Charlene's side, his forehead resting on the side of her head as he continued to whisper in her ear. "Baby girl, please. Let's go home so we can talk. Please, baby. Let's just go home."

Where the strength came from Charlene had no idea but she pulled away from him, stumbling a bit then righting herself. "No. I asked you for the truth, give it to me now."

"Charlene, we're not alone."

"No, we're not!" she yelled. "But I want to know right now what you've done. How could you do something like that? Who *are* you, Akil? Who are you?"

He straightened at that. His dark eyes going cold.

"I'll have Jax take you home," he said and walked away.

"Akil!" she yelled but he kept on walking. "Akil!" Her voice would grow hoarse, singing tomorrow would simply be out of the question, but she didn't give a damn. Everything she thought she knew, thought she felt, was a lie. He was a lie.

Chapter 19

There had been no sleeping, yet she crawled out of the bed in the room where she'd originally slept that first night in Akil's house. She showered and slipped on jeans and a T-shirt. She had one goal, one person she needed to see.

He would be in the studio, she knew that without a doubt and walked straight there. After letting herself in she didn't even go through polite formalities.

"You owe me the truth," she said, sitting in the chair across from the control board where he sat.

He wore jeans, too, and a wrinkled T-shirt, a sign that his night had been just as rough as hers.

"I owe you," he said with a smirk. "I owe everybody, huh?" He was shaking his head.

"I asked you for the truth long before your little friend entered the picture. You should have just given it to me then."

"Should I have?" he asked. "Why? Because you wanted me to? Because you asked me to? Let me ask you something, Charlene, do you get everything you ask for?"

She opened her mouth to speak but he held up a hand to stop her.

"Wait. Yes, you did. Whatever you wanted growing up you got. You didn't have to ask for shoes that had a new sole on them because you were tired of your toes sticking out in the winter. You didn't have to ask for a couple of dollars to go to the market to get milk and cereal because you and your sister had nothing else to eat. You didn't have to compete with a crack pipe or a needle full of heroin to get your mother's attention. So I guess when you ask me something I should bend over backwards to give it to you."

His words stung. The vehemence in his voice brushed coarsely over her skin. But she would not take the blame for this or anything else that had happened to him. "You can try to shift gears all you want but I gave you respect. From the first day I met you, Akil, I respected you. Even when you acted like an ass I still respected you enough to tell you. So yes, when I ask you a question—no, *correction*—when I ask the man I'm sleeping with a question, I expect an answer."

He sat quietly for a moment, his hands folded. He looked like he was thinking, possibly about a song or an arrangement. From first glance you couldn't tell the emotional battle going on inside him. But Charlene felt it, felt the deep-seated fury just itching to break free, and was afraid of what he would say next.

"What T.K. said was right. My mother was a junkie. She'd taken her first hit of cocaine straight from my father one night after he'd played at some nightclub and she'd sung. They were so excited when they came into the house late that night. I knew where they'd been so I stayed up to hear how it went. I heard their laughter and crept out of my bed into the living room. That's where I saw him dig into his pocket and pull out the little packet. He made two straight white lines on the coffee table, which was full of so much dust it was a wonder they didn't snort all that up, too.

"Every day after that she was high on something. Coke, crack, heroin, whatever she could get her hands on that could take her to the place she wanted to be. When my old man was killed I thought she'd finally have a chance to get clean, but she didn't, she just found another pusher who would keep her appropriately sexed, pregnant and of course high."

"Akil," she whispered.

He shook his head. "No. You wanted an answer, now you take it! I owe it to you, remember?"

She remained quiet, tears already burning her eyes.

"Lauren was thirteen. She needed her mother. She needed some guidance. I'd been working at this record store while I was volunteering at Empire so I was paying the bills in the house and making sure Lauren got up and went to school. While Betty was just doing her thing. I don't know where she got money to get high, probably stealing or selling herself. But I'd long since stopped putting money in her hand. I couldn't stop her from shooting up or snorting, but I didn't have to pay for it, either. She had a key to the house and a bed to sleep in every night. That was all I could do for her.

"One day the school called me, said Lauren hadn't shown up that day. I knew I'd gotten her out of the bed that morning and watched her go to the bus stop. So I left work, drove around the neighborhood looking for her, asking if anybody had seen her. Somebody said they saw her and Betty late that morning. I didn't like the sound of that so I started looking around at Betty's hangouts. I don't really remember how I ended up on Oliver Street or why I started walking down that alley. It was dirty, full of trash and old needles, broken bottles, just a mess. But I kept right on walking down that alley. It was getting dark by then and I was going to leave but I heard something coming from behind a couple of the trashcans. I walked farther and there she was."

He dragged his hands down his face, rubbed his eyes.

"She was only skin and bones by then but I recognized her from her hair, it was matted but it was long, dark. Then she opened her eyes, brown eyes that used to have these tiny flecks of gold in them. I remember when she smiled they kind of sparkled." A muscle in his jaw twitched. "She was so high she couldn't even stand up. I tried to help her up twice, asking where Lauren was.

"'You're so much better than me, Akil. You always have been.' That's what she said. I ignored her, didn't want to hear anything unless it was about Lauren. We walked a couple feet before I finally picked her up and was carrying her. She pulled on my shirt and tried to yell but her voice was just about gone. 'Save my baby,' she whispered. 'He's got her and you need to give him this to save her.'"

Charlene stood then, walked over to the control board and took his hands. "It's okay, we don't have to talk about this if you don't want to."

He shook his head and pulled his hands from her grasp. "She gave me three hundred dollars. Told me I only had an hour left to get to her, to save her. To save my thirteen-year-old sister from the drug dealer she'd sold her to for a hit."

Tears poured from Charlene's eyes and she wanted to reach for him again but his entire body had gone rigid.

"I put her down because she'd started yelling that she was in pain. 'Be better than me, Akil. Save my baby.' That's what she kept whispering while she rolled into the fetal position, pain from the bad drugs she'd been sold eating away her insides. Be better than me. She told me that. And I thought I was. So I went straight to the police station, told the desk sergeant everything Betty had told me. They packed me up and put me in the cruiser. We went to the house where the dealer was holding Lauren. They sent me in. I paid him and he pushed my sister out the door. Her clothes were ripped, her face streaked with tears. I carried her out, fighting back the need to find me a piece and kill that son of a bitch. The minute I got outside the police raided the house. Everyone inside was arrested."

"Oh, Akil," Charlene couldn't help saying. She knew he didn't want pity, knew he didn't want her tears, but she couldn't help them. The more he talked the more her heart broke for the child he'd been, the years he'd lost and all he'd tried to do.

"They just dropped us back off at home, told us to keep our mouths shut and we'd be safe. They never told us that I was the one who led them to the dealer who they'd been trying to get for years. Said they had an anonymous tip in court and watched him walk away with a life sentence for kidnapping, bartering a minor and drug charges based on what they found in the house. They knew that if word got out that I'd come to them I'd be labeled a snitch in the neighborhood and neither

Lauren nor I would make it alive another year. So we all went on with our lives like nothing happened.

"Betty died, ten minutes after I left her in that alley. We buried her the next weekend. About two years after that I found out that the drugs that killed Betty and the dealer that supplied them to her were a part of a federal investigation. They were somehow connected to a senator and his Colombian connections. But by that time I didn't even care. I never looked back. Never regretted what I did," he said slowly, then looked up at her. "Until now."

"I'm so sorry," was all she could say. "I'm so, so sorry."

"Why? You were millions of miles away living a happy life in your mansion. What could you have done to prevent it?"

She hadn't thought she'd lived a happy life but it paled in comparison to his. Her battles with weight and her fight for her mother's unconditional love were nothing compared to his fight to save his mother's life and his burden to save his sister's.

"I don't understand what T.K. wants."

"T.K. wants what everybody who didn't make it out of the hood wants, Charlene. Money. Fame. Fortune. Purpose. The life they were denied. He expects me to give it to him because he's threatening to tell what he knows about my past. I don't do threats and I don't owe him a dime."

"What are you going to do?"

He stood abruptly then. "I answered your question." His voice was tight and Charlene felt like she was once again being dismissed. "We have a few more weeks to work on the CD but I think it would be better if you stayed in a hotel while we did. Cliff will drive you. I'll leave a message with the hotel with the date and time of our next session."

She blinked rapidly, confusion blanketing her. "What? Hotel? What are you talking about?"

"I'm talking about us taking care of business. That's what we should have been focused on in the first place."

"But, Akil, what about T.K.? What about the FBI looking for you?" *What about us?* she wanted to say but had too much pride to go there.

"I'll take care of me. All I need you to do is sing. Just sing."

Chapter 20

The sound of rain tapping against the hotel's window was dismal and monotonous.

Charlene turned over in the bed, burying her face deep in the pillow. Breathing was hard this way, but not as hard as it had been since she'd left Akil's house. A part of her was still there; miles away in that secluded mansion her heart remained.

It had been three days. He'd called off all recording sessions, probably so he didn't have to see her. The first day away from him she'd thought about how she could have handled the situation differently. But how did one act when they heard the man they were sleeping with had killed another person? And when that other person was their mother? After the initial shock she'd realized the man she was in love with could never take a human life, especially not his mother's.

She'd remembered that night he'd told her about his

family and the hurt and despair in his voice when he'd spoken of his mother. He wanted her to get clean and to be healthy. He couldn't have killed her. And when she'd gone to him for a complete explanation, the one he'd given her had broken her heart.

How had he survived? How had he lived all these years knowing the moment he'd walked away from his mother in that alley she'd died? But she understood, there was nothing else he could have done. Betty knew that, so she'd sent him away to save her daughter, to save both of them. And Akil had done that. He'd walked away from his mother to save Lauren. But now look where Lauren was.

Guilt must be a constant companion to him. Heartbreak like a close relative. She cried for him, for the way he blocked his heart to anyone else out of fear. She cried for his loss—his mother, his father, his sister. And she cried because she loved him too much to just walk away. She just didn't know how to stand beside him right now.

Steady knocking at the door meant she had to climb out of this bed, to move her body when her limbs were tired from not moving much the past few days. She didn't know who was at the door but they were persistent. So she climbed out of the bed, grabbed her robe and shuffled barefoot across the room.

"It's about time. You could answer your cell phone, you know. I've been calling and calling. And so has your sister."

Marjorie Quinn came into the room like a summer's breeze. Her salon-treated auburn hair was perfectly styled, her bronzed complexion highlighted just so with expensive cosmetics. On her arm was a Chanel bag—her mother only carried Chanel bags. She wore a cream linen pantsuit and taupe patent leather pumps. Her fragrance was light, breezy, sophisticated.

"Mother?" Charlene said, a little blurry-eyed and a lot confused. What was her mother doing here in Miami? The last time she'd spoken to her had been weeks ago. Or rather when she'd called home the day after she'd arrived here she'd spoken to the answering machine letting them know where she was and that she was fine. She hadn't received a callback, which made this impromptu visit all the more perplexing.

"What are you doing here?"

"Just like I said, you haven't been answering your cell phone."

Charlene shrugged. She hadn't answered it because it wasn't the number belonging to the person she most wanted to speak to.

"I've been busy," she lied. No way was she telling her mother she was screening her calls.

"And you're not staying at the address you gave me on the message."

So she'd been to Akil's house. "No. I'm not."

"And you look an absolute mess."

That was said in the normal Marjorie Quinn "I'm so tired of going through this with this girl" voice.

"Thanks, Mother. You look really nice."

Marjorie smoothed down her jacket and gave Charlene a weary stare. "You're about to be a big music star, Charlene. Please tell me you're going to do something about your wardrobe. Your appearance. Your father and I do not want to be embarrassed."

Her words stung. Charlene was so not in the mood for this. "Is that what I've always been? An embarrassment to you?"

Marjorie shook her head negatively. "No. That's the role you've elected to play."

"Maybe because of all the pressure you put on me to be like Candis. To lose weight, to model." She was walking back and forth now, her arms flailing, her frustration clearly misdirected.

"To make something of yourself. To follow your dreams. To not settle for just anything," Marjorie finished. "That's what I did, Charlene. I pushed you to reach your potential. I never asked you to be like Candis. That was all in your head."

"In my head! The diets, the exercise programs."

"So my daughter would be healthy. Do you know how many ailments start with obesity? I never once wanted you to be something you're not. But you created that story and you've lived by it so long you believe it."

Charlene finally plopped down on the bed, the little amount of energy she'd had already gone. "Why? Why are you here now? Why are we talking about this now after all this time?"

Marjorie sat beside her. "Because you brought it up."

Charlene sighed and Marjorie took her hand. "Why don't you tell me what's really bothering you?"

Truth be told, all the stuff she'd just mentioned had been bothering her for years. But her mother was right, it wasn't foremost on her mind right now. And while her mother wasn't her first choice of who she'd like to be discussing this with, right about now she was as close as Charlene was going to get.

"How do you help someone who doesn't want to be helped?"

Marjorie chuckled. "You've said a mouthful there.

I've been trying to help you all your life and you've fought me every step of the way."

"Mom, I thought we weren't discussing 'us.'"

"Okay. Okay. Maybe we can finally discuss that later and put it behind us once and for all."

"Fine," Charlene agreed just to be done with it.

"Sometimes, Charlene, we think people need help. And if we care about that person then who better to offer that help but us? We never really think about whether or not we should help, or whether we should just leave well enough alone. You know, let the good Lord do His work, in His time."

Charlene thought about her words for a moment, wondering if they were talking about the situation with Akil or still the past disagreements between her and her mother.

"But what if you really love this person? If you only want what's best for them? If you just want them to know that you're there for them?"

Marjorie nodded with each of Charlene's statements. "But you may be the only one who believes you can help them. This person may need to find their own way, make their own mistakes or decisions."

Okay, this was paralleling too much with her issues with her mother. She was talking about Akil, trying to help him. But he didn't want her help. Would he want her love instead?

"How will he know I love him and I care?"

Her mother smiled as she tucked a strand of hair behind her ear. "Tell him."

Charlene looked at her mother, knowing definitely that what had just transpired between them was groundbreaking. It was taking their relationship to another level. "Thanks."

Marjorie held out her arms and Charlene went into her embrace. "I love you, Charlene. I love you because you're you and you were stubborn enough to fight me on everything I did or said that I thought was helping you. You were strong enough to stand your ground and become your own woman. I'm so proud of that woman. And if this man is worth a dime he'll love you for being there as well as wanting to help him."

"He's worth it," she whispered, her face resting on her mother's shoulder. Akil was worth fighting for. All these years people had been letting him down, walking out of his life, and he'd been fighting to keep them there in any way he could.

He deserved so much better. And for all that she was not model-thin or picture-perfect, she was good for him, she knew it with all her heart.

What she also knew with a major degree of certainty was that there was no way Marjorie Quinn was going to let her off that easily. The next hour was spent telling her all about Akil, about the man she loved.

Akil was pleased.

He'd just finished writing the lyrics to the song that had been in his head for much too long. Only yesterday afternoon had he figured out why the words hadn't come to him sooner.

Charlene.

It was that simple. Just as she'd said when she first heard the instrumental version of the song, it was a journey between this man and this woman, falling in love. He'd written a few songs in his career, none that he'd sold or had published, but just a few projects he'd done on his own. This one was totally different.

The woman was different and the timing was right. That's all he could figure.

He was tired of fighting demons, tired of carrying all this guilt. It was time for him to live and to love. That was basically what Mrs. Williamson had said when he'd been at the breakfast table alone yesterday morning.

"Akil, I've known you a long time. I know things about you that I don't think others know."

He'd only been able to nod, sure that whatever she was going to say would make him feel ten times worse then he already did.

"You're a good man and you deserve happiness. It's time for you to let go of all that old baggage and move on."

He'd steepled his fingers and rested his forehead against them. "That's what I was trying to do."

"Ha!" She'd yelled so loud he'd jumped. "That's not what you've been doing. You've been hiding behind work, snapping at anybody that dared to get closer than your music. It's a shame the way you treated that woman when all she wanted to do was love you."

"Are you talking about Charlene?"

"You know good and darn well who I'm talking about. She may have come here to make a record but I think it was more. I think the good Lord brought her here for something more. You're just too stubborn to see it."

He sighed. "I really don't want to talk about this right now."

"That's just fine with me," she'd huffed and sat down across from him. "Don't talk. Listen for a change. That's a strong black woman. Strong enough to handle her illness and rise above all this petty talk about skinny women being the only beautiful ones out there. I ain't never heard such foolishness. God created us all different. Beauty is in here." She had pounded against her chest with a closed fist, her light brown eyes staring fiercely at him.

"She has a lot to give and some man is going to take her up on that offer one day. It'd be a darned shame if it wasn't you."

Just the thought of Charlene being with someone else had him seeing red. His temples had throbbed with the headache he'd had since the day before when she'd packed her things and left for the hotel. He'd wanted to call her back, to tell her he was wrong and to beg her to stay.

But she would have turned and looked at him again, given him that look of pity he didn't want to see again. His past was his past, he didn't want pity for it, didn't want anybody's apologies because it wouldn't change a thing. He just wanted it to be forgotten.

Charlene wouldn't forget, she would remember and she would probably love him more because of what he'd gone through. Every day she was with him he'd wonder if it were out of pity or something else.

"She loves you," Mrs. Williamson had said quietly. "I think it's about time you stopped questioning that and just accept it. I believe you love her. Well past time you stopped running from that, too."

He couldn't speak, he only looked at her.

She had stood and gone to him, grabbing his face in her beefy hands and kissing his forehead. "Stop making me yell at you all the time. You're not a stupid boy, Akil. You're smart and talented and you should know a good thing when it's staring you right in the face. Now get up and do something about it."

All afternoon he'd thought about that conversation

and admitted to himself that Mrs. Williamson was absolutely right. So he decided to do something. He'd finish the song that Charlene had given him some lyrics to and then he'd go to her, begging for her forgiveness.

But this morning there had seemed to be too many people in his house, so he'd gone to his yacht for some quiet time before going to see Charlene. That's what he was doing when he heard footsteps on the dock.

For just a minute he thought the footsteps would keep going. Then he expected his bodyguards to stop whoever was approaching. Of course that could only happen if he hadn't given them the day off. Yeah, he knew T.K. was still around and that he wasn't going to give up his quest for the money he thought was rightfully owed to him. But Akil didn't care. He'd never run scared before and he wasn't about to start now.

Besides, it was probably just Jason. He would know where Akil had gone to get some peace and quiet. So Akil hadn't moved to the upper level, just waited for him to come down the steps to where he was.

"See, this is what I'm talkin' 'bout. I'm gonna get me one of these real soon."

It wasn't Jason, Akil thought, standing from the couch where he'd been sitting to glare at T.K.

"What are you doing here?"

"You keep asking me that question, man. But you already know the answer."

"I told you I'm not giving you a dime."

"Okay. You did say that. But I figured with our history I owed you one more chance to reconsider."

"There's nothing to reconsider," he said. T.K. stood about five feet away from him. He was wearing saggy blue jeans with a frayed hem over boots. His jean jacket matched his jeans, the Barack Obama shirt looking dismally out of place on a black man who refused to work for anything.

"It's simple, Akil, you cut me a check. Then I can even work for your company or something to keep the money rolling in. It's either that or I go to the FBI."

"Go where you want, but you won't be going with any of my money."

"You's a stingy, ungrateful, nig—"

Akil took a step closer to him. "Don't do it. Don't call me out of my name. I'm trying to deal with you like a man, T.K., but you don't want to go that route."

"I ain't gotta go your route to anything. Don't forget I saw you in that alley. I saw you leave her there. You knew she was dying, you could have saved her."

Akil's jaw twitched, the memories flashing back in his mind quick, like a trailer for a bad movie. "Yeah, you keep saying you saw me. But I didn't see you. Why is that? Huh? Why were you in that alley, T.K.? And when I left why didn't you help her?

"She fed you, washed your clothes. Hell, sometimes she had to do the same for your just-as-strung-out mother. So I'm confused. Why didn't you help her?"

T.K. was up in Akil's face now. "You don't have to bring Rosita into this. We're talking about you and what you did to your own mother. I took care of my mother until the day she died."

Akil nodded. "Yeah, you took care of her, all right. Probably put the needle in her arm for her."

"Oh, no, don't get it twisted. You're the killer, not me."

"But you were in that alley. Like you knew Betty was there, that she was high. How would you know that, T.K.? How would you know unless you were the one who sold her the bad dope?"

T.K. just laughed. "You can't prove that."

"You're right, I can't. But I know that's what happened and that's all that matters."

"But the Feds are going to get proof that says otherwise."

"You can't blackmail me, T.K."

"I can do whatever I want!"

"That's what you think. Just like you thought your no-good daddy was coming back for you. Until he picked your behind up, drove you out to the county and stripped you naked, leaving you like a piece of trash."

T.K.'s nostrils flared. His eyes grew darker as his fists balled at his sides.

"Yeah, you were real pissed off about that. He didn't want your mother, didn't even pick her up off the streets when he rode by and saw her nodding on the corners. And he sure as hell didn't want you. You were his half-breed son, half boy, half junkie—why would he want you? So you killed him. You stripped him and shot him and left him in that crack house. So which one of us is going to the Feds first, T.K.? You with your news about a junkie being left to die in an alley or me with my info on a dealer who killed a cop?"

T.K. growled in anger. With both hands he pushed Akil back. As Akil stumbled backward T.K. reached into the back of his jeans and pulled out a gun.

"I will kill you where you stand," he said, his voice deadly calm. Like a man who'd done this before.

Charlene had heard enough. When she'd stopped by Akil's house to see him Mrs. Williamson had hurriedly told her he was at the yacht and that he was probably waiting to see her. She didn't really believe that but was not going to be deterred.

At the dock she was directed to his yacht. She was walking slowly down the dock. Since she hadn't anticipated being out on the water, she'd worn a sundress and three-inch-heeled sandals. The last thing she wanted to do prior to taking a stand with Akil was to fall on one of these wooden planks and break a bone.

Then she'd heard the yelling. It was coming from Akil's vessel. She'd moved closer and recognized the second voice as T.K.'s. Wondering what he was doing there, she'd decided to eavesdrop for just a few minutes, then she'd let them know she was there.

The exchange was heated, with Akil verbally attacking T.K. for his transgressions as T.K. had tried to blackmail Akil for his. It was on the one hand disheartening to hear the tragedy of both their childhoods. When they should have banded together to rise above their situations, they'd been brutally torn apart. On the other hand, it was scary as hell to hear them yelling at each other like this and it just about stopped her heart to hear T.K. threaten Akil's life.

That was the final straw.

Using her cell phone as she made her way onto the boat and down the few steps, she alerted the police to their location.

She thought T.K.'s threat was just that. It didn't dawn on her that he might really have a weapon to carry out his plans. But the moment she stepped into the cabin his entire body, including the arm with the gun, turned and now pointed directly at her.

"I know you're not using her as your backup," he snarled. "Get over there with your man, since you picked right now to show up."

"Don't move, Charlene," Akil said in a slow, venomous voice.

She didn't know what to do. All she knew was that her heart was racing and her palms were sweating.

"Fine. I ain't got no problem shooting her first, then taking your sorry ass out." Something clicked and Charlene thought it might have been him taking the safety off the gun.

But at that exact moment Akil pounced, knocking T.K. to the floor.

They tussled for a minute but T.K. was still holding on to the gun. Charlene took another step in their direction and stomped on his wrist, over and over until his fingers finally gave out and let the gun go. That pointy three-inch heel had come in handy. She didn't want to pick up the gun but didn't want T.K. to have the opportunity to pick it up either so she kicked it out of his reach.

Akil took that moment to plow his fist into T.K.'s face. Okay, he deserved that one, she thought. But then Akil didn't stop, he kept pounding and pounding on T.K. until she could see blood and didn't know where it was coming from.

"Stop it! Stop it, Akil! He's not worth it," she said as she heard the first police sirens pulling into the marina.

Stepping around them she tried to grab his shoulders, then his arm as he went to swing again. "He's not worth it and beating him to death won't bring your mother back."

Akil's chest was heaving as he sat back on his legs. She held the right arm but his left one fell to his side. When his head turned and he looked at her she saw the weight of his world clearly in his face.

He'd felt guilty for leaving his mother to die. For years he'd lived with that guilt. He felt guilty that Lauren was on drugs and had lived with that, too. Now he felt rage, a tremendous amount of rage that she feared could lead him down the wrong path.

"It's okay, baby," she was saying, falling to her knees to kneel beside him. "It's okay now."

His head dropped, his chin hitting his chest, and he made a sound that she wasn't sure was crying or sighing. But she put her arms around him, hugged him tight and kept telling him that it was all right.

"You did what she asked you to do. You saved Lauren, that's all she wanted."

"But I didn't. I didn't save her."

"Yes, you did. Lauren grew up and made her own decisions. You can't blame yourself for that. You did your best."

"I should have done more. I should have been stronger, put my foot down, made her listen."

"No!" Charlene said adamantly, pulling back to look at him. He still had his head down so she cupped his chin and lifted it up. "She should have been stronger. Lauren should have fought harder to be different. That wasn't your battle and it's not your burden to carry now."

On the floor T.K. was moaning. Footsteps sounded on the dock and in seconds the police were busting into the cabin. Akil stood, then helped her to stand, holding her hand tightly.

The officers were cuffing T.K. and retrieving the gun Charlene told them she'd kicked to the side.

"I'm sorry," he said.

She was already shaking her head. "Don't. It's done."

"But I hurt you.'

She nodded. "You did. But I'm stronger than I look.

I'll get over it because I know you were doing it out of self-preservation."

"No matter what you call it, I was wrong. And I apologize. I love you," he said simply.

And it was enough.

She picked up his bruised hand, kissed his knuckles. "And I love you."

Chapter 21

Two Weeks Later

Holding that last and final note had felt good. The following applause felt even better.

She'd done it!

The song was titled "Journey." It was the one she and Akil had both written the lyrics to. After the episode on the yacht they'd returned to his house to be pampered by Mrs. Williamson and the staff. The FBI had come along with questions to which Akil openly provided answers. Even about his mother's death and his involvement in the impromptu sting to catch a drug dealer all those years ago.

He said he felt like he'd completely purged himself and she was happy for him. Heading back into the studio, the first song he wanted to work on was "Journey." It was a joint decision that she'd sing it tonight as she was in L.A. performing for the Pediatric AIDS Benefit Concert produced by Playascape.

There were no nerves when she'd stepped up on the stage this time. Well, okay, there were some, but they were quickly tamped down when she touched the bracelet on her wrist, the one Akil had given her. Just that action reminded her that he was in the room with her, that their hearts were now intertwined and their love strong. Singing the song, "their" song, seemed appropriate.

Afterward, the gang was all there, so to speak.

As Charlene walked off the stage, down some stairs and through a door that led to the seating area of the club, she saw them all sitting at a large table, already toasting glasses of champagne.

Jax was right beside her, helping her make her way through the crowd. A few people stopped her, gave their congratulations or comments, making her feel like all her hard work had paid off. Well, all *their* hard work, she should say.

At the table her parents were the first to hug her. She still couldn't believe they'd shown up, but as Marjorie had tried to tell her, all she'd done in the past had been out of love and concern for her child.

Candis was also back in the States, sitting a little close to Jason on the high-backed black leather couches that offered seating for one whole half of the table. After her parents, Candis had torn herself away from Jason to stand and give her a hug. "He's too young for you."

Candis only laughed. "Girl, didn't you know I was a cougar?" she said giving a mock growl.

Charlene was still laughing as Jason pulled her in for a tight hug. "You're doing the damn thing, girl! I'm proud of you."

"Thanks, Jason. It's all because of you."

"Yeah." He nodded. "I'll take some of the credit."

He was so goofy, maybe he and Candis did make a good couple after all.

"Hey, girl, you were fantastic up there." Rachel was next up, hugging her once, then again for good measure. "And you look great. Mia told me you were going to look good. I wish he was here, but he had to go to New York. You know how he is."

"I know you should have warned me about the hormone therapy before he showed up as a she," Charlene said, laughing.

"Oh, yeah, forgot about that one." Rachel laughed.

Charlene noticed the handsome man sitting right next to where Rachel had been and looked in his direction.

"Oh, almost forgot. This is Ethan Chambers."

The first thing Charlene noticed was that this brother was even finer in person. The tabloids didn't do him justice. The second thing she noticed was that he absolutely adored Rachel. The way he'd been watching her as they'd talked said it all.

"Hi. It's nice to finally meet you, Ethan."

He nodded and shook her outstretched hand. "Same here."

"And this—" Rachel took her hand from Ethan's and walked her a couple steps toward the end of the table "—is Olivia Blake. She worked on the set with us at *Paging the Doctor* and now she's signed up with Limelight."

Wow was Charlene's first thought. *Tall, mocha-skinned* and *gorgeous* were the only words she could think of to describe Olivia.

"Livia, please. And you sounded great up there."

"Thanks," Charlene said, shaking her hand also.

"So, listen, Ethan and I are getting married at his brother's winery."

"What? Married? Did I miss something?"

Rachel looked from Livia to Charlene. "Oh, no! I told you. I know I told you, Char. I had to."

"You didn't, but we can talk about that later. So you're getting married at a winery?"

"Yes, his brother has this great winery in Napa Valley. The perfect setting, right? So, anyway, I want, no, I need, both of you to help me plan this thing because you know I don't have a clue."

"She's been talking like this for the last couple of days," Livia explained to Charlene.

Rachel was getting married? "Sure, you know I'm there for whatever you need."

"Okay, so how soon can you be in Napa Valley?" she asked.

"Who's going to Napa Valley?" Akil asked, stepping up behind Charlene and wrapping an arm around her waist.

"We are, to plan a wedding," Rachel said, practically beaming. "So you have to give my girl here some time off so she can come and help me."

Akil looked at Charlene and was all smiles. Since leaving his yacht that day and watching the police toss T.K.'s begging behind into the patrol car she and Akil had been inseparable. And their relationship—the personal one—was now common knowledge. Everybody who had eyes and were blessed to be in their presence knew they were in love and Charlene was ecstatic about it.

"A trip to Napa might be nice for both of us," he said, then dropped the sweetest kiss on her lips.

"Hmm, we might be hearing more wedding bells soon," Livia chimed in.

Everybody was talking and laughing and having a good time. Everybody except Sofia.

Charlene had talked to her briefly before going onstage but she had yet to see her since finishing her performance. She was curious to hear what she thought of the song and the sound of the CD, but she didn't see her.

She'd just left the table and was headed to the ladies' room when she spotted Sofia and the guy Rachel had told her earlier was Ramell Jordan, head of A.F.I. Ram, as Rachel said he liked to be called, who was also a good-looking man. Only Sofia probably wasn't thinking that right at this moment.

From Sofia's defensive stance and the sway of her neck as she was speaking, Charlene was guessing that whatever those two were discussing wasn't good. She figured she'd better get back to Rachel and let her know. It looked like they'd be planning some sort of intervention for Sofia and her workaholic status some time in the very near future.

Akil owned a penthouse in L.A.'s South Park district. Here, in stark contrast to his Miami home, was all about what money could buy. Spacious, decorated in sharp black, silver and gray tones, each room spoke of elegance.

Charlene didn't not like it, she just liked the Miami house better.

They'd been back from the concert for about an hour. She'd changed into her nightclothes as it was almost one in the morning. Akil still had on his slacks but had shed the jacket and button-down shirt he'd worn earlier. He was sitting at the piano that she hadn't known he could play. Going over to sit on the bench beside him, she noticed it was a Steinway grand piano and whistled.

"Really nice piano. I didn't know you could play," she said.

His fingers were moving idly over the keys and a quick melody echoed throughout the room.

"I can do a little somethin', somethin'." He smiled and she leaned against him.

"You're very talented, Mr. Hutton. I think that might be one of the reasons I love you so much."

"Oh, really?" He played a little more. "So it has nothing to do with my charismatic personality?"

"Nah," she said, playing along with his good, joking mood.

He nodded. "Good, because I thought it was more about the way you seem to hit all the high notes when you're with me."

That made her blush but she didn't back down. "That's certainly a high point. But that's not it, either."

He stopped playing and took her hands in his. "I can tell you why I love you so much."

No matter how many times he said the words her heart still fluttered at the sound. "Why?"

"Because you're you. Never once were you afraid to just be yourself. I had no choice but to fall in love with Charlene Quinn, the woman, the singer, the friend."

She smiled at that and he was rewarded. There was no need for her to say the words to him; he knew how she felt. And he was content just having her here with him. Finding Charlene was the best thing that had ever happened to Akil and he vowed never to mess that up.

The doorbell rang just as he was about to tell her they should retire for the night.

"Don't tell me you planned an after party?" she joked.

He was already standing and walking toward the door. "I didn't, because I wanted us to share this part of the celebration alone. So if it's Jason with more champagne I'm leavin' his butt right in the hallway."

But it wasn't Jason, as Akil saw quickly upon opening the door. She was about thirty pounds smaller than the last time he'd seen her, but he'd know her anywhere. They had the same eyes, the same strong chin. She fidgeted with her bag, looked down at her feet then up again at him.

"Hi, Akil," she said in a raspy voice. "Can I come home, I mean, can I come in?"

His heart was too full to speak. When he felt Charlene's hand on his shoulder he could only nod.

"You must be Lauren," Charlene said, extending a hand to the pretty young woman standing nervously in the doorway.

Lauren nodded and shook Charlene's hand.

Akil finally cleared his throat. "Of course you can come home, Lauren." When she had released Charlene's hand he took a step forward and pulled his sister gingerly into his arms and hugged her tight. "I've missed you so much," he whispered in her ear and felt his life was now more than complete.

He had his sister back and he had Charlene, the love of his life.

* * * * *

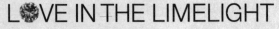